NIGHT SHADE

MELISSA CUMMINS

Melissa Cummins

Cover by Mayhem Cover Creations
Editing and Proofreading by E.M Editing
Formatting by Melissa Cummins
Published by Melissa Cummins on September 28th, 2021
https://melissacummins.com/
ASIN/ISBN: 0578987430/9780578987439

Contents

Dedication.......... 5
Author's Note.......... 7
Chapter 1.......... 9
Chapter 2.......... 15
Chapter 3.......... 21
Chapter 4.......... 31
Chapter 5.......... 39
Chapter 6.......... 45
Chapter 7.......... 57
Chapter 8.......... 67
Chapter 9.......... 81
Chapter 10.......... 93
Chapter 11.......... 107
Chapter 12.......... 113
Chapter 13.......... 125
Chapter 14.......... 135
Chapter 15.......... 145
Chapter 16.......... 157
Chapter 17.......... 165
Chapter 18.......... 177
Chapter 19.......... 187
Chapter 20.......... 197
Acknowledgements.......... 211
Author's Bio.......... 213

Dedication

To my husband, even though you're not a vampire, I'd still choose to spend eternity with you.

Author's Note

Night Shade is a friends to lovers, betrayal, gamma hero, soul mates, paranormal romance novel. It is the first in the Chronicles of The Otherworld series. Each novel will always contain a Happy Ever After (HEA) for the couple. All of my works occur in the same universe so you will see the characters mentioned in other novels and even other series.

Chronicles of The Otherworld is intended for mature audiences. This story contains mentions of physical, emotional, mental, and sexual abuse, drug use, suicide, violence, explicit language, and sexually explicit scenes.

Reader discretion is advised.

1

The mattress squeaked underneath them. Sweat glistened off Daniella's skin as she rode Alexander, working them closer to ecstasy. Alexander gripped her hips hard as he fucked her, bruising her skin, slamming into the slick heat of her body. She knew he was close. Daniella ground her hips in response, her eyes drifting shut as her head fell back. No longer did she see the pale man beneath her, with his curly, sandy hair sticking to his forehead, and his heated brown eyes. Instead, he shifted in her mind, changing into the one she truly desired. Her fantasy lover. It was his silky brown hair, his darkened eyes, his smell, his taste.

Yes, yes!

His was the body beneath hers, filling her, bringing her closer to climax.

The familiar shiver started at the base of her spine, circulating throughout her body, and then it snapped hard, making her cry out as she came. In three quick strokes, Alexander joined her with a loud, guttural moan.

Daniella draped her long legs over the edge of the bed. Her orgasm left her feeling warm, relaxed, until the man behind her stirred.

"Another go?" Alexander smirked as he thumbed a new condom.

She cringed. Her stomach knotted, a deep weight settling within as her intuition flared to life. It demanded he leave. If it weren't for the few glasses of liquor she'd had before he called, she would have never allowed him into her home.

Daniella stepped away from the bed to retrieve her robe. "No, I've got to get ready for work."

Alexander purred. "It could wait."

She could feel his eyes as they roamed over her form, like a slithering snake ready to strike. Daniella narrowed her eyes. "No, it can't." She lifted her curled brown hair from the collar of her robe and tied the sash tight around her midsection. "I'm sorry if you're confused, but nothing about our deal has changed. I came, you came, and now it's time to go. I have things to do, and I'm sure you do as well, *elsewhere*."

She breathed a sigh of relief when Alexander's feet hit the floor. She turned to give him privacy while he dressed, but her body refused to relax.

He's leaving. Just give him a couple of minutes.

Daniella pressed the button to open the long drapes covering her floor-to-ceiling windows. Her gaze settled on the breathtaking view from her penthouse floor, unobstructed by the surrounding New York skyscrapers. The soft rays of the sun were low against the horizon, but still magnificent in the way their rosy tints contrasted through the early morning blues.

A noise behind her shattered her serenity. Daniella turned and found Alexander there, still naked and much too close. She took a step back, and he took another forward, caging her against the glass. He smirked as he tipped her chin up, his lips hovering near her own. "Now come on, Daniella, we both know you didn't mean no."

She snapped at his unwelcomed advance and slapped his hand away. But before she could speak, he covered her mouth and pressed against her. "Or do you just like it rough, pet?"

Her fight-or-flight response went into high gear. Daniella opened her mouth and bit his hand, hard. Alexander chuckled at the pain as if it were nothing, but he pulled back just enough to give her an opening. Daniella used the space to twist, and then flew forward as she threw a punch at him.

Alexander dodged, jumping back. He threw up his hands, but that asinine smile was still on his face. "Alright, I'll go. No need to be so hasty. But just remember, I'm only here because you agreed to let me in. I don't know why you're playing hard to get now when I was deep inside you not even ten minutes ago."

"And I think it's hilarious you think it's an act." She glared at him, clenching her fists. "You're right, I let you into my home, but you know what? Everyone makes mistakes they wish they could take back. So, let me be perfectly clear since you didn't understand the first two times. You have two choices. Either you leave my house willingly, or I will haul you out myself."

Alexander let out a low whistle and backed away, grabbing his clothes and shoes. "Whatever you say, babe. Whatever you say."

It wouldn't go away. The nagging, soul-wrenching feeling that something was wrong had buried itself deep in Daniella's gut. If she was being honest, the feeling had been there for the past two weeks, but not this intense.

Before, it was a whisper, something she could turn a blind eye to. It didn't worry her; it wasn't even a blight on her day. But today, everything felt drenched in the icky, sinking blackness. Even after her cup of coffee, warm bath, and meditative session, she still felt filthy. Perhaps the situation with Alexander had bothered her more than she'd realized. He'd never acted that way before. But today … Daniella shook her head. It didn't matter. She would never see or speak to him again, and if he tried anything, she could always rely on the guards in the lobby.

Daniella blocked his number, and on her way out she had a quick chat with both security guards. Under no circumstances was he to enter her floor, or the building, without her authorization. After confirming she was all right, they replied with a sincere, "Of course, Miss Ismania."

Despite that, the feeling remained. If her intuition was right, she was in for a hell of a day. With a sigh, Daniella managed to thank the guards before she scurried out the door and set off to work.

2

The Novak Firm was Daniella's home away from home. She loved her work, the company, and most of all, the people. Yet the moment she entered through the double doors, she almost vomited.

Panic and dread crept up her spine, making her shudder. She labored her way to her office and stashed her breakfast in her mini refrigerator. Several keystrokes later, her inbox confirmed her fears. The executive team was to meet in Conference Room B immediately for an emergency meeting. Taking a deep breath to steady her nerves, she made her way to the room, pen and paper in hand.

The moment she opened the door and saw Luke's face, some of her tension eased. Luke had been her best friend for the last four years. They met in college as dorm neighbors and bonded over their differenc-es. She appreciated his out-of-the-box thinking, creative spirit, and how it directly contrasted with her analytical and serious personality. He loved to laugh, to make others smile, to throw caution to the wind. Luke taught her how to have fun, how to balance her dedication to work while still appreciating life. He'd introduced her to his cousins, Gregori and Mya, and they had embraced her as if she was a missing part of their family.

When Luke told her that he and Greg wanted to start a business, it didn't surprise her. But when he asked her to help with their accounting part-time, she'd nearly fallen out of her chair. Wanting to support her friends, she said yes, but she never imagined that decision would have put her on the path to becoming the CFO of a now multi-million-dollar agency.

"Good morning, sunshine," Luke said with a small smile.

"Good morning to you too." She paused, taking in his ruffled copper hair and slightly wrinkled clothing. "Is it still going to be a good morning after this meeting?"

"I wish I knew, Dani. I wish I knew."

Before she could respond, the door opened behind her and the air rushed out of her lungs. Her nerve endings awoke, firing so fast that goosebumps erupted over her skin. She shivered from the sudden change in body temperature and bit her bottom lip to keep from gasping. The expansive energy washed over her and spread throughout the room—dark, hot, seductive. Daniella didn't need to see who was behind her. There was only one person who had ever made her feel this way.

"Good morning, Ella." The deep baritone of Greg's voice rolled over her in waves.

She straightened in her chair, trying to disguise her body's natural response to him. "Good morning, Greg."

He walked to the head chair, coming to stand between herself and Luke. While he conversed with Luke, she looked him over. Gregori Novak was breathtaking. He was a six-foot-six Adonis covered in toned bronze skin that made his Spanish heritage proud. His russet-colored hair fell to his ears, complementing his sharp jaw and strong facial features. While Greg considered his eyes to be brown, she had stolen enough glances at him to know they were, in fact, hazel. They took on a life of their own, becoming lighter or darker depending on his mood, sometimes even light enough for her to see their pale jade depths. They drew her in, enticed her, while his lips could—and often did—convince her of anything. And if that wasn't enough, he also had a perfectly shaped ass.

Luke cleared his throat and she blushed at being caught ogling. The door opened once more, saving her from any additional embarrassment.

Once the rest of the executive team arrived, Greg took his seat, drawing their attention. "Now that you're all here, let's begin."

The room fell silent when Greg uttered the single word "embezzled".

"Embezzled? What the fuck do you mean, embezzled?" Mya snapped.

His eyes narrowed. Mya's anger was second to none and she was about to unleash it in full force. "Mya—"

"Do not 'Mya' me right now. How the fuck did this happen?"

"We don't know. But this is a time for solutions, not anger."

"I go away for two weeks, two fucking weeks, and this happens?" she grumbled.

Greg's eyes bore into Mya's, warning her to keep her mouth shut. She sat back in her chair with a frustrated sigh, crossing her arms while still glaring in his direction. That was as good as he would get, and he'd take the small blessing.

He scanned the room, observing his team. Merida and Dominick appeared cool and collected, even though he knew they were brimming with anger inside. Luke had also known of the news prior to the meeting, which was the only reason he hadn't lashed out like Mya.

Greg's gaze lingered on Daniella, who concerned him the most. Her amber eyes stared down at the table, unblinking. She may have hidden it well, but the death grip on her pen told him exactly how upset she was. She took her job seriously and was devoted to not only the company, but his family as well.

"Aren't there accounting principles and security measures in place to prevent things like this from happening?" Johanna asked. "I'm sorry, but I'm with Mya. I don't understand how this could have occurred."

As his Chief Human Resources Officer, Greg knew she had a right to this table. He could understand her concerns, especially if anything might affect funds for wages and benefits, but he did not appreciate her subtle accusation of blame toward Daniella and Merida.

Merida took control of the situation, her voice taking on a professional tone. "That's an excellent question, Johanna." She laced her fingers together. "The security and accounting protocols that we have in place are why we made this discovery so quickly. This is a jarring and confusing time for all of us, but we will collaborate with the pertinent parties to find the perpetrator and fix any security issues in our processes. If you have any questions regarding this incident, please be sure to come to my office and I will do my best to explain everything to you."

"Thank you," Johanna responded, giving Merida a curt nod.

Greg continued, holding the gaze of each person around the table as he spoke. "I know this is a stressful time for everyone. Your behavior here shows how much you care about this corporation and the dreams that Luke and I founded this company upon. We thank you, and are confident that we will overcome this setback."

He motioned to his security team. "Merida and Dominick's team will be speaking with each of you and your departments. We trust that if you have seen anything suspicious, you will be forthcoming with any information you may have. As Merida has already stated, if you have any questions, please direct them to her. Thank you."

Greg watched as Daniella stood, her expression tight as she left the room. Johanna followed after her, leaving him, Mya, Merida, Luke, and Dominick behind.

The moment the door shut, Mya sat forward, her lips curled. "Now that the fake bullshit is over, tell me what really happened."

3

Greg paused outside of the door to Daniella's office, his fingers clutching the brass handle. *You have to. Just keep it together for a little longer. Remember, you're keeping her in the dark to protect her. She can't know, not yet.* He took a deep breath, rolled his shoulders back, and stepped into her office.

Daniella froze, her fingers mid-key press. Trepidation flashed across her face when she saw him, and even though it was only for a moment, it made his heart ache.

Greg cleared his throat against the emotion as he closed the door behind him and shut the horizontal blinds. "I didn't mean to startle you."

"No, it's all right." Her voice was tight, clipped, and he hated it.

Greg sighed. "Ella, come here."

They met in the middle, somewhere between him reaching out to pull her into his embrace and her curling herself around him. “It’s not your fault.”

Daniella trembled in his arms. “But it is.” She lifted her face from his chest. “It’s my job to make sure that the company’s finances are squared away, and I failed. Someone stole money from here, from us!”

She moved away from him and began to pace, her hands flying in the air as she spoke. “I’ve been backtracking through all of my reports, trying to make sure this has never happened before. What if I missed something? What if that’s the cause for all of this? They got away with it once and thought they could again?”

He took her flying hands in his own. “Ella, this is not your fault. You are brilliant and an incredible accountant. Because of you, we know exactly how much was taken. If your reports were not as detailed as they are, or if your data was not up-to-date, we would be screwed.”

She looked away, but Greg grasped her chin, forcing her to look at him. “Give yourself some credit. You saved us. You, no one else. I see it that way, we all do. None of us blame you, and I’m not going to sit here and let you blame yourself either.”

Her gaze drifted downward as she shook her head. “I just don’t know, Greg, I just don’t know.”

“Well, I do,” he replied with a tap on her chin.

Greg let his hand drop from her face, and he led her to her conference chairs where they sat facing one another. Daniella tucked a strand of hair behind her ear, then sighed. "Thank you for comforting me, but you're the one who had their money stolen. How are you doing?"

"I'm okay. Disappointed, but okay."

"But how are you so calm? Why aren't you angry or frustrated?"

Greg rubbed the center of his forehead. "Because someone has to be. Luke was only calm because he knew beforehand. Without that, between Volcano Luke and Hurricane Mya, someone would have lost their head."

Daniella hiccupped a laugh, clamping her hand over her mouth to keep the sound contained.

He chuckled at how effortlessly adorable she was and then forced himself to mask his emotions. While she thought he was joking, he wasn't. Before he came to her office, Greg had to stop Mya from going on a murderous rampage against their nemesis. She wanted retribution for the chaos that monster had caused, and so did he. But right now, all he wanted was to see Daniella laugh, see the way her mocha-colored eyes twinkled in delight, and how her shoulders relaxed as the stress left her body. He wanted his mate to be safe.

"I'm sorry, I'm sorry. It's just, those two are something else. I don't know how any of you survived to this age," she said with a smile.

"It was difficult, I can tell you that."

Daniella leaned back and crossed her arms, studying him. "Greg, there's something you're not telling me.

What are you hiding that kept me from finding out about the embezzlement before that meeting?"

His lips wavered. "Sometimes you know me far too well."

"Maybe, but I also know when you're trying to change the subject. What is it?"

Greg ran his fingers through his hair before clasping his hands together. He slouched forward, elbows resting on his knees. "A security alert was released early this morning. Since Mya was on her way back from her vacation, she didn't receive the notification, but her team and the security team did. They looked into the matter quickly and found that the bank transfers were initiated internally. Both teams scanned the system three times." He paused as his gaze met hers. "The credentials that were used to log in last night and trigger the alert were yours."

Daniella gasped. "What?"

"Ella, we know it wasn't you. But the person who did this, they were smart. They left almost no trace. Even Mya is having a tough time tracking them down, but they left that information, which means they did it on purpose."

"Oh my God!" Daniella squeezed the bridge of her nose as she held her face in her hands.

He leaned forward and stroked her forearm. "Hey, what did we say? This was not your fault. I need you to understand that. A competitor could have done this. You are one of the founding pillars of this company, so it wouldn't have been hard to get your name. Our entire team's roster is up on the website."

"But my fucking credentials aren't!"

"No, they're not, which makes me think it was an inside job."

"I don't leave my credentials lying around the office, Greg," Daniella bit out.

"I know you don't. The problem is anyone on the IT or security team with enough know-how could have stolen them. We're a growing company. We're interviewing and filling positions that we have never had before."

"So, it could literally be anyone?"

He nodded. "Yes. I have an idea of how to figure this out, but I need your help."

Daniella looked up at him. "Greg, whatever you need, just ask me."

"I need you to take a vacation."

Her eyebrows rose. "I'm sorry, what?"

"There are only so many reasons someone would want to go after you here, one of which would be to steal your position. If you were gone for a couple of weeks, that person would think things were working in their favor. Then they'd start rumors, try to help more than necessary, and we would find out who's really responsible."

"Case closed."

"Exactly," he replied, nodding. He could see the wheels turning in her head as she pondered the plan.

“Greg, if you think this will work, I’ll do it, but it doesn’t feel right to me. Why go this far just to get me fired? There are plenty of easier ways to try. It feels like they’re not only going after me, but the company as well.”

“I don’t think they’re only after you, either. But I do think you’re a part of their plan and this was the only way they could try to get rid of you. You can’t reason with someone’s irrational logic, and we won’t know exactly what is going on until we catch them.”

Daniella took a deep breath. “Okay. I’ll stay out of the office for a few weeks. But I’m going to monitor every transaction that comes in or out of the corporate account. While I may cooperate with this ruse, there’s no way I’m letting the accounting get that far behind.”

Greg smiled as some of the tension left his body. “Yes, ma’am.”

Anyone who watched Greg walk out of the elevator and down the hall—his steps measured, back straight, head held high—would think he was having a nice, calm day. But that calm was a practiced lie. The moment he shut the door to his office, the deep-seated rage and need for justice flooded out of him. His fingers curled around the mahogany desk, tightening to the point that he left impressions in the wood.

Breathe, he commanded himself. *Breathe before you lose it.*

Today was a nightmare, and it wasn’t over yet. As the president of this company, it was his job to make sure that he appeared professional at all times. But as the current leader of the Novak Clan, the reigning circle of vampires in the Northeast United States, it was his duty to be ready at every moment. He did not get peace, he did not get pity, and when his people died, he took it personally. Greg carried the weight of his title with his muscles tense and ready for battle at every turn, and now they sensed a new opponent charging towards his door.

Luke stormed into his office, shouting a millisecond after the door had slammed against its frame. "Gregori, what the hell do you think you're doing?"

"Lucas," he warned, but his cousin was clearly in a red haze and did not understand how close Greg was to losing control.

"You sent her away? What the fuck is the matter with you? How could you ever believe she's the reason for any of this?"

Greg's anger was feeding into his power, his need to unleash, to break, to destroy. He counted backward from one hundred, trying to tune out the accusations.

"Did you not see how hurt she was? None of this would have happened if you had taken the proper steps to ensure her safety!"

That was it. Greg's eyes flashed red. "Enough!" he shouted, slamming his fist so hard the wood of his desk buckled from the blow. His power surged around him like a shock wave. The room darkened, shadow seizing light as Greg's powers expanded and grew. The black was so dense that it prevented entry from the sun's strong rays.

Luke froze, his mouth hanging open at the rare explosion.

"Do you think," Greg bit out, "to question my judgment?"

"Most days," Luke replied, his retort earning him a growl.

Greg closed his eyes again. *Breathe in, breathe out.* He balled his fist and called his power back to him. His family meant everything to him and he would never hurt them, but there were times when they pushed him too far. He could only take so much, and today was not the day to test him.

As Greg spoke, the glowing red of his eyes dimmed. "Let me connect the dots for you, Luke. Daniella's credentials were used to log into the system."

Luke's eyes narrowed. "I already know that."

"Then let me tell you something you clearly missed while you were busy berating me. They left them there on *purpose*. The attack on our finances was done directly after the attack on our people, by Zachariah. Not because he needed the money, but because he knows, Luke. He knows Daniella is my mate."

His cousin gasped. "That's impossible, the only people who know—"

"Work in this building." Greg rubbed the corner of his eyes and sighed. "They're the only people who have seen us together, and only an immortal would have been able to sense our connection. We have a mole, Luke. Daniella is not safe here, nor is she safe at her home. That is why I sent her away."

"Greg—"

He shook his head. "I know how much you care about her, and you know how I feel about her as well. But we lost twenty-two people last night from the attack." Greg clenched his fists again. "I have already failed those people. I am responsible for their deaths, and I will catch Zachariah, and I will enjoy watching the blood drain from his body. But Daniella…" He shuddered at the thought. "I will never, ever risk her life or her safety. I can't."

4

Daniella kept her head down as she exited the building. She'd been successful in avoiding everyone until she ran into Luke at the elevator. She told him about Greg's plan, knowing he'd be upset if he wasn't included. He was quiet at first—never a good sign with him—but when his jaw ticked, she knew he was about to erupt.

She tried to explain it to him once more, but it was like talking to a brick wall. Luke could be over-protective and wasn't one to change his mind, especially not when he was seething. He cursed under his breath and stomped out of the elevator towards Greg's office. She felt bad for Greg and the whirlwind barreling in his direction, but if anyone could handle Luke, it was him.

She sent Luke a quick text to call her once he'd calmed down, and then another one to ask him if he'd grab her laptop and drop it off at her house tonight. It killed her to leave it there, unattended for the afternoon, especially after her credentials had been used, but she needed to keep up the ruse of a questionable probationary period. She tried to convince herself that they would find the perpetrator, but the task seemed incredulous.

Go home and relax. Take a nice long bath, order an extra-large pizza, and drink a tall glass of chardonnay. That's all you can do right now.

Yet the thought of her home made Daniella's stomach tighten.

Glancing at her watch, she realized it was afternoon. She hadn't eaten all day. Once she had some food in her, she'd feel better. That was the only thing that made sense.

Daniella stopped at a little corner café and ordered herself a delicious steak and horseradish melt with a generous portion of avocado, and a raspberry lemonade. She chose a seat outside, where she could enjoy the warm sun and cool breeze. Nature always helped to put her back on balance. But when she thought of going home again, her stomach cramped so hard she almost vomited.

What was going on? She'd never felt this way before. And to be this sick, especially all day? She knew not to disregard her feelings. How many times had her foresight helped her to avoid the worst? But this? Now? Her home had always made her feel safe, so this had to be something else.

Instead of going home, Daniella stopped in every store she could think of and even took a trip to the museum, trying to enjoy the many sculptures and extravagant paintings. But then the sun began to set, and when she checked her watch it was after 6:00 p.m. Luke usually left the office around this time, and if he'd got her message, he'd be on his way over with her laptop. Thinking of him made her feel better. Maybe she'd entice him with the pizza and he could stay and have a bite.

Maybe I should call and ask him to pick me up? Daniella shook her head at the ridiculous notion. She was fine, everything was fine, and yet with every step closer to her home, she felt worse.

With her building in view, she heard the familiar soft tones of a violin. Daniella appreciated the opportunity for distraction and turned past the topiary and towards the melody's creator, Stacy.

Her friendship with Stacy had begun strangely. Stacy played outside of tall complexes and skyscrapers, handing out flyers for her performances to anyone she could. She always went for the "big fish" and had figured Daniella to be one. But somewhere between Stacy's over-energetic and pushy nature, and her beautiful way of enthralling someone with her music, Daniella had grown to love her, even if she hadn't been given much of a choice. Stacy simply felt good to be around. She was a positive force in Daniella's life, but the moment her eyes landed on Stacy's small blonde form, bile sputtered from her mouth and she turned to vomit into a bush.

Stacy ran over to her and placed her hand on Daniella's back. Instead of comfort, Stacy's touch felt like daggers piercing her skin. Daniella pulled away as more bile and unrecognizable chunks spat from her mouth. *It's never been this bad.*

"Dani, are you okay?"

"Yes," she gasped, begging her stomach to stop dry heaving. "I-I'm fine," she lied. "I think I have the stomach flu. I'm sorry for worrying you. Go back to playing, I'm okay."

Stacy reached for her. "Dani, you look horrible. Come on, let me help you—"

"No!"

Stacy pulled back and Daniella stumbled to her knees. She wiped her mouth with the back of her hand, eyes watering as she looked up at Stacy. "The stomach flu has been going around the office. I guess I'm its next victim." She braved a laugh, but Stacy still seemed skeptical. Daniella noticed her clasp her hand tightly to her chest, as if she'd been stung or wounded. "I'm sorry, did I hurt you?"

"No, no. I've probably just been playing too long. But are you sure you're okay? I can help you back to your house?"

Daniella winced at the instant headache brought on by the mention of her home. "No, it's okay. I don't want to make you sick too. Plus, someone will try to take your spot if you're not here."

"Yeah, they're a bunch of vultures." Stacy sighed, turning to check and make sure that no one had touched her violin or taken the money she'd collected. Then she shifted her focus back on Daniella. "I am going to watch you and make sure you make it into your building, and when you get upstairs, take some medicine and call me after you've rested a little, okay?"

Daniella smiled, but shook her head when Stacy offered to help her up. "I've got it."

She stood and closed her eyes for a moment. Taking a deep breath, she focused on her mother's mantra, one of the few traditions she had left of her. *I am one with the earth. I am one with the Mother. She flows through me. She offers me her guidance, and I can make it through anything.*

After the third time, Daniella opened her eyes to Stacy's puzzled face, her crystal blue eyes clouded with concern. "I'm feeling better. Don't worry," she said, hoping she sounded convincing enough.

Stacy mumbled something in German and rolled her eyes. "I will always worry about you. You're always working. You don't take care of yourself." She threw her hands in the air. "I work on the street and I'm healthier than you. If I find you passed out in front of your building, I'll call an ambulance for you, only after I knock you upside the back of your head."

Daniella gave a real laugh this time. "Yes, mother. But you may want to save that for the man getting a little too close to your money."

Stacy turned and stomped towards the stranger, all five-foot-three of her yelling in a mixture of English and German.

Daniella shuffled to her building, counting the steps. Anything to draw attention away from the familiar blackness. The war between her physical body and whatever was bothering her intuition was so intense that she felt lightheaded. Opening the door to her building, she looked around for the night guard, but his post was vacant.

That's odd.

Stacy played right outside of her building, and she had been shouting obscenities. He must have gone to make sure that everything was all right, meaning Daniella had missed him by the time she made it to the door.

Her stomach lurched again and she rushed to the elevator. She scanned her keycard, entered, and felt triumphant the moment she pressed the penthouse floor. She'd made it!

Slouching against the golden mirrored wall, her relief was replaced by a buzzing under her skin, as if a second beat had started in her heart, renewing her strength. Her body flooded with a mixture of bliss and energetic adrenaline, and for the first time she questioned if everything that she'd felt had been some sort of anxiety attack, or a mixture between that and her normal intuitive feelings. After all, she'd had a horrible morning, barely eaten, and had been on edge for the entire day. Perhaps what she'd believed was her intuition was really an ugly ball of fear and stress, and she had simply made herself sick. Maybe she really did need to take a vacation, get out of town for a couple of days. Maybe Stacy was right. Maybe she was overworking herself.

As she touched the handle of her apartment door, it shocked her. Daniella wrung her hand from the zing of static electricity and tried again, her fingers still tingling from the jolt. This time, the handle moved and she entered her home. Yet, instead of feeling relief, a fresh wave of dizziness hit her so hard that she rushed towards the half bathroom in case she was going to hurl. Her body stopped mid-motion, held back by something she couldn't comprehend. She tried again, but to no avail.

Someone chuckled behind her, and her hair stood on end.

"Oh, Daniella, I'm not going to let you get away that easily. I have to punish you for making me wait."

5

Daniella gasped. What was Alexander doing in her house? She had made sure he left this morning. How did he get in here?

"What the fuck are you doing in my house?" She thrashed, trying to break out of his hold as he tightened his arms around her from behind.

"Not so fast, sweetheart." He grabbed her chin, forcing her head to the side. "You love to think you're in control. It's a bad complex that you have, really, but you're not, nor have you ever been."

Daniella squirmed and fought against him, but his arms held her in place. No matter how hard she tried, he was unmovable.

Her heartbeat thundered in her ears. *Calm down and think!*

He was stronger than her, so she had to be smarter than him. She had to wait for her chance. Daniella couldn't reach her phone, and no one would hear her scream from here. He would give her an opening, eventually. She just had to wait. By then, Luke would find them and she'd have an ally in her fight. Hopefully. She just had to wait.

Keep him talking, act scared. "What do you want?"

She felt Alexander shrug behind her. "It depends on the day. Some days it's world domination, other days to feed, others to fuck, and, occasionally, to take everything away from my enemies. I appreciate you for assisting with all of them."

Daniella shuddered. World domination? To feed? *What the hell is wrong with him?* "You're sick."

He snickered. "No, I'm driven. Besides, you only have yourself to blame for the situation you're in." His hand slid over her breast and he squeezed it hard.

Daniella's body recoiled in disgust.

"If you had let me get inside of that thick head of yours earlier, I would have spent the rest of the day fucking you. Then, who knows? I might have been able to spare you. But alas, you were too stubborn for your own good." Alexander purred. "Although, there's no reason I can't have fun with you before I rip out your throat." He bent his head to her neck, sucking at her skin.

Daniella held back the bile that rose in her throat. *Just a little more,* she told herself.

His hold on her torso loosened as he moved his hand to grip her through her pants.

Now! She bent forward and then snapped back as hard as she could, slamming the back of her skull into his nose.

Alexander yelped and his arm dropped. Daniella fought against the dizziness and stumbled toward the door, but she wasn't fast enough. Before she knew it, he grabbed her by the neck and slammed her against the wall so hard she saw stars.

"Oh, I'm going to enjoy this," he said, and when her eyes focused, she could see a smirk playing on his lips.

The door to her home blew apart. Alexander swung her around, using her body as a shield from the debris. Daniella's heart stopped when she saw the cause. Greg. He looked furious and his eyes were … red?

Greg moved toward her but stopped when Alexander tightened his grip on her neck.

Alexander tsked. "Now, you wouldn't want me to break your mate's neck, would you, Gregori?"

Mate? She didn't have time to focus on the word as Alexander's nails dug into her throat.

"Let her go," Greg demanded, his voice low.

Alexander chuckled. "I don't think so. That was never going to happen, not when I found out this tasty little morsel was your mate. She's quite delicious, really, and a fantastic fuck."

She could see the wheels turning in Greg's mind. Daniella wanted so badly to reach out to him, to connect with him, her salvation, but she knew she couldn't, not until she was free of Alexander's grasp.

His grip tightened again, forcing her to gasp for air. She tried to claw Alexander's hand from around her neck, but her eyes filled with tears and her vision clouded. Even though she couldn't see Greg, she could feel him. Her body responded to his, nerve endings firing under her skin even as breathing became difficult. She fought recklessly, struggling, gasping, writhing to break free.

Please, I don't want to die here.

Greg snarled, and a dark, deep-seated rage filled her. Something crawled beneath her skin, ripping her apart. The chains of her consciousness rattled until they snapped, and a single certainty filled her mind. She would not die here.

"Ella!" Greg yelled.

Daniella's hands fell from Alexander's grip around her neck as her body hummed with energy. "Let me go," she choked out.

Alexander laughed. "This one's a handful! She really thinks she can take on a vampire. Cute. Does she know that you and your little family are vampires? How weak and pathetic you all are? You've spent centuries trying to stop the vampire wars when so many lives could have been saved, including hers."

"I said, let me go!" Purple sparks of electricity shot out from her, attacking the thing that held her hostage. She no longer saw it as a human, no longer recognized it as a lifeform. She wanted it to bleed, to suffer, to no longer exist in this world.

Alexander screamed, throwing her away from him as he fell back against the wall. Daniella clutched at her throat, coughing, spasming with each new full breath.

Greg leapt onto her attacker. They tumbled and hissed, curses and growls coming from their tangled bodies that moved much too fast. The blurs careened back and forth, crashing against the walls and into objects, shattering glass and wood, denting metal. But then their bodies flew, smacking against the glass in such fury that it shattered and the blurs were no more. They had fallen out of her window and into the night.

Her vision darkened and she collapsed with one final thought. Alexander couldn't have survived that fall, and neither could Greg.

6

Daniella shifted under what felt like an enveloping cloud. She was so warm, so comfortable in the weighted softness that she never wished to leave. But her mind pleaded with her to open her eyes.

When she did, she saw two forms in the darkness. They were speaking in hushed tones so low she couldn't hear. One opened a door and light illuminated their silhouettes as that of a man and a woman. Immediately she felt safe, loved; they were familiar to her. Yet, when she tried to lift her head to greet them, it pounded with such violence that she fell back onto the pillow and groaned.

"Dani?" a familiar voice said. "Hey, hey!" They rushed to her side and pressed on her shoulders. "Don't try to get up, okay? I don't want you to pass out again."

Even though she heard and understood what the voice was saying, she tried with more determination to rise. Something important had happened. If only she could fight through the pain to understand, to remember.

Please stop, Daniella begged the pounding in her head, and her eyes grew wide when it did. *What the fuck?*

She heard the soft click of a light and shielded herself from its luminescence. Once her eyes adjusted, she could finally see the face beside her. "Luke?"

His shoulders sagged. "You remember me, that's good."

Daniella shook her head, smiling. "Of course I remember you, silly. Why wouldn't I?"

And then she remembered everything else.

Her mind shattered into a million pieces, just as the glass in her apartment had done when Greg flew out of it.

"Greg," she hiccupped, a sob trapped in her throat. "He … He—"

Luke smiled and patted her hand. "He's fine."

"No, I saw him. Luke, I saw him!"

"Shh." He squeezed her arms. "Who do you think brought you here?"

"But he couldn't—"

She clutched at her chest. Her body shook, pulsing unnaturally as the room swayed in and out of focus. Alexander had said they were vampires. Vampires weren't real. They were nothing more than a fairytale. But Greg couldn't have survived that fall unless…

She stared at Luke, wide-eyed. "He's…" She gasped as realization hit her. "You're all vampires."

He grimaced. "Dani—"

Static electricity surged around her. "Please get away from me."

"Dani, please, let me explain—"

She struck out her hand. "Stay away!" The walls seemed to be closing in around her. Gasping, she pleaded, "Please, I-I don't want to hurt you."

Luke nodded, taking several steps back until he stood in the middle of the room. "Just breathe, okay? Inhale and exhale. You can do it, Dani."

But she couldn't. The room felt heavy, out of focus, spinning out of control. She closed her eyes, clutching at her chest. It was an anxiety attack. She used to have them as a child after her mother died, but it had been so long ago that she couldn't remember all the steps to calm down.

Breathe, she commanded to no avail. She clawed at her skin, begging her body to pull in more air. But each breath felt stale, unmoving, like sucking in cement.

The door slammed open, the noise so loud that it shocked her. A gust of cold air was the only warning she had before strong, warm hands squeezed her arms.

"Ella." Greg's voice pulled at her, connecting to something beneath the panic, something strong, wild, "It's okay, everything is okay."

He's here! Daniella chanted internally, but her mind couldn't rationalize it. How was he here? Confusion changed to fear, and she began to lose control.

"Get away, please. Something's wrong." She clutched at Greg's shoulders, but he wouldn't budge.

"Listen to me. Look at me." He cupped her chin.

Daniella obeyed, her eyes meeting his own, and it felt as if he was peering into her very soul.

"You're not going to hurt me. Whatever is going on, whatever this is, release it."

"Greg—"

"Let me help you. Trust me, Daniella."

He leaned so close that she could smell his unique scent, spicy wood wrapped in cinnamon and musk. Her eyes drifted shut as she breathed him in, trembling. When she breathed out, the room blew apart.

A window exploded as air forced its way in, whipping around her. Large vines traveled through the opening as if they had a mind of their own, winding around furniture and electronics, crushing them, breaking them apart under their heavy weight. They poured and poured and poured so fast, until they suddenly stopped.

Daniella gasped, drawing back and taking in the carnage she had caused. In less than three seconds, she had destroyed everything.

This is impossible. How could I have done all of this? Her eyes darted as her skin grew pale. *This can't be real, there's just no way–*

She gasped. "Wait. Luke. Where's Luke? He was here when—"

"He's fine," Greg interrupted. "He came to get me when you started having an anxiety attack. Do you feel better?" he asked, rubbing her cheek.

Daniella splayed her arms wide. "Greg, look at what I did!"

"But do you feel better?" He smiled, cocking his head to the side.

She couldn't figure it out. Was he really here, kneeling in front of her, smiling, after everything that had happened? But she knew how those hands felt against her skin, how connected she felt to him when their eyes met, how he made her feel safe. A million different people could act, look, and seem like him, but there was something deep within her that would always know the difference.

Daniella took another deep breath, letting his warmth seep into her skin. She stared into Greg's eyes, searching for answers to questions she couldn't comprehend. They were jade now, reminding her of a pale moonstone, and yet glowed from within with a power she could almost feel.

"He hurts for you. Hunts. Protects. He waits," voices whispered to her.

Daniella drew back. She searched for whoever, whatever, had spoken to her, but couldn't find the source. As strange as it was, the voices soothed her panic, leaving a welcomed feeling of reassurance.

"He waits," they said again.

Greg frowned. "Ella? Are you okay?"

She needed to be here at this moment. Whatever this was, it would figure itself out along the way and she would get a handle on it in time. Daniella bit the inside of her cheek. "Is it weird if I say yes?"

Greg slumped forward, a small smile teasing at his lips. "Not at all. It's been a weird day." He stood and lifted her in his arms, cradling her to his chest.

She squealed at the sudden movement and wrapped her arms around his neck. "What are you doing?"

He chuckled. "Exactly what it looks like, carrying you."

Daniella scowled. "I can walk, you know."

"Not barefoot on vines and broken glass. Plus, you don't know your way around here yet."

They emerged from the room into full light and her mouth fell open in awe. Floor-to-ceiling windows covered an entire wall, providing a glorious view of the mountains. *Mountains?* She gripped his shoulder. *This isn't New York City. Where am I?*

She took in the walls, paneled in a deep royal blue that reflected the warm light from the golden sconces. The ceiling lights behind them dimmed as those ahead brightened, activated by each step Greg took. Turning her head over his shoulder, she could see a black ornate banister that wrapped the landing and led downstairs just before Greg shuffled her into a new room.

This room had a similar ambience—dark yet warm. The walls were painted a walnut brown. As he moved, she took in two doors—both closed—a black dresser, matching nightstands, and a large bed with a black padded headboard. Greg pulled the bedcovers back with one hand and then laid her down with care.

She sighed and let him pull the covers over her, but when he went to move away, she stopped him. "This is your house, isn't it?"

His gaze flickered away from hers, but then he nodded.

Daniella's eyes narrowed. "I thought you lived in the city."

Greg squatted beside her. "I kept this house off record so that anyone who stays here will be safe."

"And what happened to me earlier happens so often that you need to have a safehouse?"

"I know of this place, my family knows of this place, and now you do too." He moved his hand, holding her own, rubbing his thumb over her skin. "I just want you to be safe. That's all I've ever wanted."

"I suppose I should feel special," Daniella said sharply, "but, I'm beginning to understand just how much I don't know you at all. I didn't know where you lived or what you were. Are you even thirty?"

He winced.

"Right." She pulled her hand away from his, but he reached out to grab it again, trapping it between his palms.

"Ella, I know. I know I hid things from you, but that was never my intention. It was never what I wanted."

"And yet you did it anyway. Greg, we have been friends for years! I thought I knew you, and now I'm finding out that I don't. I just went through the worst experience of my life with someone who is apparently a complete stranger to me. How else am I supposed to feel? You lied to me, not once, not twice, but multiple times. How am I supposed to trust you?"

He cupped her cheek. She desperately wanted to pull away from his warmth, to let him know it wasn't that easy. But it was, and that made it even more infuriating.

"I never, ever wanted to lie to you. I never wanted to hide anything about myself from you. It has been one of the hardest things that I have ever done, but I did it to protect you."

Daniella scoffed, rolling her eyes.

"I'm serious, Ella. What happened to you today could have been much, much worse, and it happened to you because of me," he croaked. "I know you don't understand that right now, but when I explain everything, you will. I have to live with that on my conscience. I failed you. All the lying and hiding I've done didn't stop that from happening. Knowing that will bring me more despair than anything else in this world."

She gazed at him, at this strong man who seemed so vulnerable right now. She desperately wanted to believe him, to forgive him. But she couldn't, not without honesty.

"I asked you earlier today what you needed from me, and now I'm asking you, what do you want from me? How do I know everything you're saying isn't just pretty words, Greg?"

"Because you know me better than anyone." He tucked a strand of her hair behind her ear but froze at her bitter laugh.

"Then you clearly have some work to do."

"Maybe you're right. But I am being honest with you, right here, right now. Yes, I'm a vampire, and there's a past filled with history and knowledge that comes with that. I didn't give you the opportunity to learn those things about me, and that was wrong of me." He sighed. "But that's all they are. Things. They're just pieces of who I am. Do they make up a part of me? Yes, of course. But you … I've never been like this with anyone but you. I have to be calm enough to make decisions, to protect my people, and to do that I have to leave my heart out of it. But I can't do that with you. I can't leave my heart out of it."

He kissed her hand, making her skin tingle. Greg stood, staring down at her with a saddened expression. He had never looked so lonely. The feeling washed over her with such strength that she had to grip the side of the bed to keep from reaching out to him.

"I'm sorry for the hurt that I've caused you and for betraying your trust. I understand if you can't see me the same way you used to, or if you can't trust me again, and while I will do everything I can to fix this, I understand it's not enough. The only thing I'm asking of you is to let me resolve this situation. After that, I'll leave you alone, if you wish. Please, rest, and when you're ready, come downstairs and I will explain everything to you."

"Greg—" Daniella called out to him, but he was already gone. She groaned and laid back on the bed, staring up at the ceiling.

Vampires.

Tears gathered in her eyes, but she forced them back, refusing to let them fall. He wasn't the only one who had betrayed her. Luke and Mya had done so as well. Her friends, people who had become her family, had lied to her. They'd broken her trust, and that hurt pierced through her heart, leaving a wide hole. Yet, the thought of not having them in her life was worse.

Leaving them had never been a possibility for her, and everything in her fought against the thought of it. She struggled, battling between the hurt they'd caused and the love she felt for each of them. The happy memories they'd had, birthdays they'd spent, the company's grand opening, the times they'd laughed, the times they'd cried, how they cared for one another, how they'd cared for her, was that all a lie too?

Daniella shook her head, knowing it couldn't have been, especially not when she'd known them for so long. There was some semblance of truth there, and she held onto it like a lifeline.

No matter how angry she was at Greg, Luke, or Mya, they meant everything to her, and did she really have a choice in the matter? The man who attacked her was a vampire. These people, her friends, were vampires, and she was a literal natural disaster in the making. They were the only stable thing she had, the only ones who knew what was going on.

The emotional and mental toll the news had taken on her left her exhausted. She needed to rest, to reset herself before she approached anyone. Arguing was not the right path to truth, and she wouldn't accept anything less.

Rolling to her side, Daniella took another deep breath, inhaling the scent of spicy wood, cinnamon, and musk. The scent of Greg. This was his room. It fit him, she decided, with its warmth and darkness and how it stayed hidden away from the world. But she was here, wrapped in its depths, and—much like Greg—she would only stay if he shared his secrets with her.

7

The room was still dark when Daniella awoke. It took her a moment to remember this wasn't her house, or a place she was even familiar with, but she was safe.

The small amount of rest had served its purpose, giving her enough of a reprieve to focus on the questions circling in her mind. What did she really want? What was most important to her right now? How could she wrap her mind around all of this? All questions she needed answers to before she approached Greg.

Following the small amount of light that filtered through the curtains, she discovered the balcony and took a seat outside. But the lack of skyscrapers, foot traffic, honking of cars, or scents of street food just served to remind her of how little she knew. Taking a deep breath, Daniella did her best to accept her new surroundings and this situation. She listened to the soft sounds of birds chirping in the background as animals foraged in the brush and nearby woods, and eventually she saw the peace of this place.

A light knock caught her attention. The silly little girl in her heart jumped at the thought of it being Greg. She wanted to hold him in her arms. Hadn't she almost lost him, or was jumping out of a twenty-story building a regular walk in the park for a vampire? But her skin didn't tingle and her body didn't feel alive like it did when he was near. The disappointment she felt made her heart ache.

"Come in," she called out.

After a few steps, Luke came into sight, carrying a plate of food. "Are you hungry?"

Daniella nodded and took the plate from his hand. "Thank you."

"You're welcome," he said as he joined her on the balcony.

They sat in silence for a moment before she spoke. "I'm sorry for earlier."

"It's okay. Greg told me what happened. I'm happy he was there for you."

"He tends to do that a lot, doesn't he?" Her tone was sharp.

"It's his way. Dani—"

Her eyes bore into Luke's. "You should have told me. I know you all believed this was the right way to protect me, but it still hurts."

"I'm sorry, Dani. I really and truly am."

"How much do I not know, Luke?"

He winced.

"A lot then. Got it." She sat back in the chair, picking at pieces of her sandwich.

"Dani, there is a reason why Greg thought this was the best way to go about things, and why I agreed with him."

She snickered and then opened her mouth, ready to ream into him about how much it hurt that they didn't trust her, but she stopped herself.

Give him a chance to explain before you bite his head off. He's at least willing to give you some information, but you can't get answers if you won't listen.

Luke sighed. "Vampires are broken into sectors depending on how many are in the community and the leaders they select."

She nodded quietly, digesting the information as she took a bite of her sandwich.

"Most leaders can only manage a few hundred, others a thousand or more. They're sectioned into different jurisdictions by states, or state clusters. However, as it stands today, Greg is the leader of the Northeastern Circle, the largest circle of vampires that exists within America."

Daniella gasped and drew back in shock. "What? How?"

He stared into her eyes. "Because of how he is. Greg turned us, me and Mya, and as time went on, we took in others. Merida and Dominick, for example."

"They're vampires too?"

He nodded. “They are. If it weren’t for Greg, they would be dead right now and their baby Iris wouldn’t be here.”

Her gaze shifted downward. She was grateful for the actions that kept all of them alive today, but the news still shocked her. How was Greg responsible for all of them, and how many vampires were under his reach? Millions? How did he keep them a secret? How did he not lose his mind?

“Leaders are elected because they lead, Dani.” Luke leaned back against his chair. “Greg doesn’t just manage the firm, he manages everything. He has bought countless houses for vampires to live in, created businesses, and established full corporations just to make sure that they have jobs. He’s even vouched for mates to the council.”

Sensing her confusion, Luke clarified, “They’re like our government. Normally they sit on the sidelines, but every so often they cause chaos, and Greg deals with them. He does a lot. Greg does more good in a year than most people can in a lifetime.”

Daniella’s heart beat erratically at the news. It was all too much, especially for one person to bear. What had he sacrificed? Who took care of him when he was busy protecting everyone else? She gasped as the answer hit her. No one. No one knew him, not really. That was his sacrifice.

“But that … takes a toll, eventually.” Luke stared off into the distance. “I give Greg a lot of shit because he’s constantly doing things for other people but never for himself. But the only person—the *only* person—who he will drop everything for is you. He almost did when he fell out of that window."

"But h-he … Why did he?" She swallowed against the mounting panic in her chest. "He looked okay earlier. Is he okay? Is he hurt? I should have—" Daniella made to get up and leave, but Luke stopped her.

"He's fine. We heal faster than you do, and even faster than normal vampires."

She shook. "But—"

He stroked her arm. "He's fine, I promise. My point in telling you all of that was to explain how important you are to all of us. We all care about you, *especially* Greg. But unfortunately, that makes you a target. That's why we tried to hide everything from you, and that's why Zachariah went after you."

"But I don't understand!" She threw her hand to the side. "He told me his name was Alexander. How would he know to go after me? Why am I important to Greg?"

Luke sighed. "He may have told you his name was Alexander just in case you overheard some information and put two and two together, but Zachariah is his birth name. He's been around for a while, not as long as we have, but long enough, and he's been a thorn in our side the whole time. Zachariah's a determined fucker, but he's also smart and difficult to kill. Unfortunately."

She steadied herself against that information, forcing herself to be open-minded about a world that spoke so easily about killing someone. But then she remembered how badly she wanted Alexander's—Zachariah's—hands off of her, how she didn't care that he was a living being. She'd wanted him dead, and a part of her still did. To judge Luke, or anyone else, would make her a hypocrite.

Luke twiddled his thumbs, pressing them together repeatedly before exhaling into his clenched hands. "Zachariah went after you because you are Greg's mate."

There's that word again. "What? What does that mean?" Daniella cocked her head to the side. "Is that like a soulmate?"

"Sort of. Vampires and other species"—at her raised eyebrow, he smiled—"yes, there are others, have genetic rules. Much like humans, we can have sex, but we can't procreate nor share our immortal essence with anyone unless they're our mate. Since vampires are immortal, watching the people we love die over and over hurts, so every vampire searches for their mate. You are Greg's."

Was that why she'd always felt so connected to him? Why she'd grown to care about him so deeply? She bit her lip. How many times had she fantasized about them being more than just friends?

"What does that mean for me?" Daniella asked.

He shrugged. "Nothing really. You're not a vampire, although based on the random magic you produced earlier, you're probably a witch or something like that."

A witch? She shook her head, unable to even think about that possibility right now.

"But either way, you're not governed by the same code we are. You're free to do as you wish," Luke explained.

"And Greg?"

"Being a mate, or finding your mate, doesn't make them automatically fall in love with you." He stared at his hands. "It's a delicate process. Human mates can reject their immortal one if they choose to. They just won't share that special connection with anyone else. For the immortal though, it's an entirely different process."

"How so?"

Luke's face grew grim. "Imagine your worst heart-break and then amplify it by one hundred. That is what the immortal will feel. It's a pain worse than death."

Her eyes widened. "What?"

"Yeah, I suppose that was nature's way of controlling our population."

Daniella shuddered at the thought and then blocked it out. She couldn't deal with that level of cruelty, not now. Not ever. She forced herself to focus on the conversation once more. "But how would Zachariah know that I'm Greg's mate?"

"He'd know the moment he saw you and Greg together. The two of you are like magnets, constantly attracting one another. Someone else who had seen the two of you together could have also told him."

"But that would mean you have a mole."

Luke drummed his fingers on the chair's arm. "That's what we're trying to figure out. After the embezzlement, Greg realized Zachariah knew about you. That's why he asked you to go on a vacation. He thought keeping you away from the office would keep you safe since it was a clear, direct attack against you. Unfortunately, he was wrong."

"I knew there was more to the story, but I would have never thought this was the reason," Daniella said, letting out a long breath.

"I know you're upset that we lied. I know you wish we would have told you about this before. But honestly, how could we? Would you have believed us if we'd walked up to you one day and said, 'Hey, I know you barely know us, but we're vampires, and we'd love it if you could spend the rest of eternity with us. What do you think?'" Luke pressed at the corners of his eyes before facing her.

"Vampires tried to be open about their existence before and that resulted in wars founded on humans' fear. And while I have a much higher regard for you than that, this is a lot of information. So, we did what we could." He shrugged. "We focused on taking care of you, keeping you safe, and protecting you as much as possible. Knowing that you were in real danger gave us a huge reality check."

A violent shiver ran down her spine as Daniella remembered what happened in her penthouse apartment. Zachariah mocked and toyed with her, held her hostage in her own home. She'd been stupid to believe she could save herself from that. What would have happened if Greg hadn't come to save her?

"Dani? Are you okay?" Luke reached out to her and squeezed her shoulder, zapping her back to the present.

"Yeah, I'm fine. I just realized how much danger I was in earlier. Greg saved my life and I..."

Never even said thank you, she finished internally.

"I'm sorry. I wish—"

She squeezed his hand in return. "No. Please don't. I asked for honesty and you gave it to me. I have so many other questions, but I assume I'll need to get those answers from Greg, won't I?"

He nodded. "That's where I leave you two." Luke patted her hand. "But before I go, Dani, you're one of the best people I know. It makes me happy that I can finally share these secrets with you, even though I hate the circumstances. It's a lot all at once, so just breathe through it and follow your heart, okay?"

He took a deep breath. "I know some things may have changed about how you see us, but for us, they haven't. I want you to be happy, to feel safe and treasured. I want you to smile, and whatever makes you feel that way, even if you decide not to speak to me tomorrow, will be something I support. I will support you, always."

Daniella hugged him. "Luke, I'm confused, shocked, and still pissed off"—she slapped his shoulder—"but I'm also curious. You guys are like a family to me. You're the brother I never had. Plus, I could never hate you. You would pester me until we became friends again."

Luke laughed. "Damn straight."

"It's going to take some time. I have a lot to learn and I feel like I'm still playing catch up. But I still love you with all your ridiculousness. Just keep being honest with me, okay? I'm in this now, so don't try to take me out."

He grinned. "You got it."

8

Daniella paused at the base of the stairs to take in her surroundings. The front door was large, made of solid wood, and in a black frame similar to the windows and balcony doors. A lamp cast a yellow glow over the space from a hallway, and the same motion-triggered lights lit her path as she walked. The place was vast and open, with columns and furniture sectioning each room into its own unique space.

The foyer had a bench and a small table to the side of what she assumed was a coat closet. Daniella could imagine Greg sitting on the bench, lacing his snow boots before braving the cold weather. *Do vampires get cold?*

The living room was filled with paintings of different styles from different time periods. The heart of the room was a gigantic fireplace covered in one continuous slab of black marble. There was no TV or apparent electronics, just a grand piano in the corner which faced more breathtaking views of the mountains. She didn't know Greg played the piano. *I guess when you're immortal, you have time to pick up new skills.*

But each room, each color, each piece of furniture and its placement, said something about Greg. He said she knew him emotionally, and even with everything that had happened, Daniella thought that was true. This place felt like his real home, more personal and lived-in than his apartment in the city. It was filled with antiques and artifacts that spoke directly of him and his interests. She wanted to know more, wanted to compare the details to see if she'd find the same version of Greg she knew at the end of all of this.

Daniella turned down a hallway lined with vibrant art pieces. Arched built-in shelves held delicate sculptures made of clay, bronze, marble, and polished gold. Her eyes flickered to them, but it was the man she found inside the next room who captivated her. Greg stood shirtless, staring out of a window. As she crossed the threshold, his back tensed and rolled. The tendons in his neck became more pronounced. He turned his head to acknowledge her presence, but otherwise stayed silent, as if bracing for the worst. It took everything in her to resist the urge to wrap her arms around him and breathe him in.

"Can we talk?" she said quietly.

His jaw ticked. "Of course."

She took a seat on his blue velvet couch. It was comfortable under her body weight, and the motion provided a much-needed relief from the tension threatening to snap between them.

He joined her with a harsh breath. “Ella—”

She held up her hand, stopping him. “Wait, please. I need to clear this up with you first. Greg, I’m not happy that you lied to me. It hurt me, but only because I care about you. This thing where you and Luke think I’m going to hate the two of you and never want to speak to you again, it needs to stop.”

She reached out to grasp his hand, needing to erase the distance between them and reestablish their connection, whatever it may be. “People learn about one another as time goes on, right?”

“Right.” He exhaled and some of the sorrow in his eyes dissipated when he smiled. Greg kissed her hand, causing a jolt to race up her arm and settle in her chest, easing her worry.

“I want to learn about you, Greg. About everything, all of this,” she said softly. “Maybe I won’t agree with some things, and maybe I will, but I am in this now whether you’re ready for me to be or not, and so I want to know.”

Daniella twined her fingers through his and he embraced her hand in kind, his thumb caressing her skin. Her heart felt full of him. “You all have always been there for me. You’ve made my life more … colorful. I’m not just going to give that up because I’m upset with you, especially when I can’t fault you for what you’ve done. After all, it’s not like I told you I could electrocute vampires, did I?”

They shared a small laugh.

"No, no, you didn't. But I don't think you knew before either," he replied.

"But I knew I wasn't exactly normal. I have a strong intuition. I can always tell when something bad is going to happen, but I can't always connect the dots." She looked down at their linked hands. "To be honest, I'm not quite sure whether it's a good thing or a bad thing right now."

Greg kissed the inside of her wrist, drawing her gaze there. "Vampires have different abilities, and as they get older, they get new ones. One day they're used to the life they have, and the next their world is turned upside down and filled with chaos. But eventually, they master it by being understanding and offering themselves kindness and compassion. You just need to master this new shift in your reality, and you can do it. I know you can."

Daniella blushed at his belief in her. "Thank you. Those were some very wise words there, Mr. Novak."

He chuckled. "I do what I can. I have a friend who specializes in helping people with their abilities, and I think she can help you. If you're okay with it, I'd like to call her and see if I can set up a meeting between the two of you."

"I'd like that. Thank you."

Greg nodded. "You're welcome."

They grew quiet again, sitting together in an awkward silence. Greg's eyes were downcast, leaving her with the opportunity to look him over. While he was here physically, it felt as though his mind were miles away. His shoulders tensed and bowed, weighed down by some invisible force that she didn't know.

She sighed. "Greg, what is it?"

His fingertips froze on her skin, so she moved hers instead.

"We're trying honesty today, remember?" she pushed.

"It's not that. I'm just trying to figure out how to say this, to help you understand."

Daniella squeezed his hand. "Don't. Like you said before, I know you on an emotional level. I'll understand what you're trying to say."

His eyes flared to life with hope, much like a bird rattling against its caged door. But then, with the flip of a switch, it died down to a thin flame and left a pained darkness that broke her heart. "Before you came down here, my mind was in a million different places, focused on what everyone needs, including you. I need to finish fixing your room. Your clothes and items are in there and I want you to feel at home here. I also want to be more open with you, but there's just so much." He shook his head. "What you said hit me hard, but it's a little difficult when you've been stuck in your ways for over seven hundred years."

"Seven hundred?" she exclaimed.

Greg smiled and half shrugged. "Give or take a few decades."

"Damn, I didn't realize I liked them that old."

A laugh rose deep from his gut. The vibration spread throughout his body, down their linked hands, and over to her. She couldn't remember the last time she heard him laugh like that, but she craved its richness and how its joy transformed his face.

Greg rested his arm on the top of the couch, bending it at the elbow to support his head with the side of his hand. "You've never said that before."

"What?" she mimicked the motion, resting the side of her head against the couch.

"That you liked me."

"I mean, you're all right," she teased.

"You're not too bad yourself." Greg chuckled.

"I do a little somethin' somethin'." Daniella shimmied her shoulders and he laughed again. There was something in his eyes now, like rays shining through the clouds. *Hope,* she realized. He was hopeful, open, embracing something here, committed to whatever magic they were spinning together in this moment. She had to take advantage of it, to get the answers to the questions she needed so he could understand him, so that he could truly believe she wanted to.

"Can I ask you some questions?"

Greg smiled. "Of course."

"Where are you from originally?"

"Spain. That was my mother's homeland. She met my father, Henry, there. He was Dutch-English, but we mostly took after my mother, Eleta."

"That's a beautiful name."

"Thank you." He ran his fingers over her hand again. "The plague had spread to small villages, such as ours. Countries were pointing the finger at one another, blaming each other for the plague, and I was conscripted into their fight. While I was gone, my father fell victim to the plague, then Amani, Luke's mother, and lastly, my mother. Mya and Luke did the best they could for her, but they were too young and it wasn't a responsibility they should have had to take on."

Daniella knew that feeling, how it could warp a child's persona, contributing to lasting trauma. It was terrible, and she felt for him and his family. No one should have to watch their parents die, much less in such horrible circumstances, and to know he never got to say goodbye devastated her. She inched closer to him and kissed the hand absentmindedly trailing circles on hers. "I'm so sorry."

"It's okay. It was a long time ago." His voice was thick with emotion and he had to clear his throat to continue. "There was a rumor that someone found a cure in one of the nearby villages, so I went, hoping to get it for Mya and Luke. But there wasn't a cure. Men were spreading that information to lure people there and steal from them. They attacked me and left me for dead." He breathed out slowly. "That's where I met Lord Erik Devereux, a vampire who resided in England. He took pity on me and turned me, and then I turned Luke and Mya before they died from the plague."

"That's—" She stopped herself, wanting to focus on the positive. "I'm happy he saved you."

Greg smiled, but it didn't make it to his eyes. "Me too. He taught us how to be vampires, the fun things, what our new duties and responsibilities were. We stayed together for a long time, but he … lost someone very dear to him and decided not to live on."

Daniella remembered Luke's words. *Worse than death.* She shivered at the realization that Lord Devereaux had lost his mate.

Greg frowned. "I'm sorry. I wish those tales were more pleasant. Life was just harder back then."

"No, it's just … You have all been through a lot."

"We have, but it hasn't all been bad. I could show you some of the good times, if you like."

She cocked her head to the side. "How?"

"One of my abilities allows me to pull memories from a person. It also allows me to share my own with them. Like seeing a vision through another person's eyes."

Daniella bounced on the couch. "Yes, please! That would be amazing!"

He chuckled at her eagerness. Letting her hand go, Greg cupped her cheek. He leaned forward until his forehead was almost touching her own.

Daniella's breath rushed out of her lungs as he neared her. "Greg—"

His voice dropped to a graveled whisper as he caressed her skin. "Don't worry, I won't do anything unless you want me to."

Goosebumps spread over her flesh and she suddenly found it difficult to swallow. Daniella's lips parted as she forced a breath into her now heavy chest. The action drew his gaze and he licked his lips.

Greg murmured something as her eyes drifted closed. His breath tickled her lips, and for one glorious second she thought he would finally kiss her. But instead, he rested his forehead against hers. Something wrapped around her, a pressure that made her hair stand on end. The energy spun around the two of them like a cocoon of fine silk, and then his memories played behind her eyes.

The first was a vision of three children. *Mya, Luke, and Greg.* They were playing, throwing bits of mud at one another, rolling around until they were covered head to toe in the thick substance. A woman yelled from the doorway. Based on her golden skin, long, flowing, dark hair and resemblance to them, it must have been Eleta. She was beautiful, even more so when she laughed at how dirty they were.

The scene changed to a tavern where Mya, dressed in outlandish clothing for what appeared to be the Victorian era, worked as a bartender. Luke, the ever-present playboy, had a lady on each arm while Greg sat at a table, speaking to a man. *Erik,* she realized, based on Greg's love for the man—a cross between a father figure and a good friend. His cream skin contrasted with Greg's warm tone.

Erik's silver eyes gleamed as he leaned towards Greg and whispered, "That sister of yours is about to cause a scene again."

The direction of the vision changed as a man stood a little too close to Mya. He whispered something he must have thought was flattering, but based on how

Mya punted him clear across the room, it clearly was not. The patrons stopped and stared as if Mya had grown a second head, but she simply shrugged and yelled, "Who wants another drink?" Everyone cheered, and Mya graced Greg and Erik with a large smile.

The next visions came one after another: a tiny English cottage that they'd called home, followed by the moment they set sail to America. The purity of those memories was evident, but the love they'd shared as a family touched her the most.

The vision faded as Greg sat back, and when she opened her eyes to meet his own, they were glazed over with unshed tears.

"Thank you for sharing that with me."

"Thank you for wanting to see them." He blinked a few times to clear his vision, but his voice was a deep rumble as he spoke. "It can be so easy to forget the good times. Days can blend between one another and sometimes they seem … endless. It's good to remember." As his fingers left her cheek, they brushed against her shoulder-length hair. He tilted his head to look at something and grunted. "I didn't realize they were that deep."

"Huh? What?" Daniella tilted her head to the side.

"The marks that bastard made on your neck." His fingers traced over each one and her heart beat faster. "Do they hurt? Do you have any other injuries?"

She wanted him to continue his inspection, to undress her, slide his hands over her, under her, inside her. She wanted to feel him everywhere, to drown out everything, anything, from before.

Focus, Daniella chastised herself. To keep her hands from reaching out to him, she felt around her neck and found the four indentations made by Zachariah's nails, and a fifth on the other side of her throat. "I'm sure I do, but when I woke up, I asked my body to stop hurting and it listened. I haven't felt any pain since."

Greg hissed. "Those are going to turn into some nasty bruises."

Daniella groaned. "Fantastic, just one more thing to remember him by."

Greg froze. The tendons in his neck tensed and his Adam's apple bobbed as he swallowed. "I know I don't have a right to ask you this, but seeing your physical injuries made me think about other, deeper ones you may have. I want to help you. If you need it, that is. Zachariah said the two of you were together before, and—"

Daniella laughed at his nervousness. "There is nothing for you to ask or worry about there. I'm fine, that wasn't…" She paused and felt her face grow warm under his quiet scrutiny. "Zachariah and I had been together before, yes, but we weren't in a relationship—"

"Oh." Greg's eyes narrowed as he spoke through clenched teeth. "I see."

Rejection and jealousy flickered over his features until dejection settled over him, and she hated it. He had been all she'd ever wanted for so long. Did he really not know what he meant to her? Of course not. She'd never told him from fear of losing him or making things awkward between them. But now, if there was a chance, she had to try. She had to fix this.

"No. I don't think you do." Daniella shifted against the couch and took a deep breath to settle her nerves. "Sometimes, being around you is too much for me. I … Fuck," she croaked. "This is harder than I thought it would be."

She wrung her hands, then sighed loudly. *Just say it.* "I want you, all the time. It's ridiculous and all-consuming. Even when you're being distant, or you're states or even an entire country away, and you call me on the phone for us to talk about our days, it drives me crazy. I know we've only ever been friends, but I-I can't help how I feel," she sputtered. "And lately it has gotten to a point where I needed to resolve my … desires so that I didn't throw myself at you like a wild animal. I needed to scratch an itch temporarily. That's all that was. There were no feelings, no emotions, nothing." She breathed. "And there never could be with anyone else but you."

When she finally looked at him, she saw a boyish smile on his face, but his eyes showed something else: a deep-seated intensity and hunger that made her heart pound. She couldn't take that look. The way it shot through her, setting her body on fire as if it had just awoken from a long slumber. And awoken it had—her nipples peaked under her clothes and the inner walls of her vagina clenched with need.

He still hadn't said a word, hadn't moved a muscle. He just stared at her as if he were taking her in, savoring every word she'd said.

This is too much. I can't. She shook her head and crossed her arms over her breasts, creating a safety net for herself. Her confidence may have resembled a piece of straw in the wind, but she'd fake it if she had to. "I don't think I've ever seen you speechless before."

Greg chuckled, but his voice was so low that it sounded like a growl. "That's not why I'm being quiet, Ella."

"Then why are you?"

"Because"—he hooked his hands under her knees, dragging her to him until he was seated directly in between her thighs, making her gasp—"it's taking every bit of my control to not rip off your clothes and bury myself so deep inside you that you won't know where you end and I begin."

She panted, breathless. His skin was warm and firm under her palms, and she could imagine how it would feel to have him moving within her, on top of her, below her, consuming her, making her his. She wanted to be his. Before she could stop herself, she moaned.

Greg gripped her thighs and his hands slid to her hips as he pulled her until there was no space left between them. His eyes turned the molten amber of a raging fire, and his erection rubbed against her, seeking what she was so desperate to give.

"Then do it."

9

Never had Greg been undone before, left so open, so helpless, and then tantalized and set ablaze with such honesty. How would it feel to caress her silky skin? Was it just as soft on her breasts? Were her nipples as dark as her soft brown hair? He hoped. By the gods, he hoped. How would she taste? He salivated at the thought. What of her blood? How rich would it be as it flowed into his mouth, as he bit her, mated with her?

He rubbed her cheek, following the line down her jaw to her neck. Then he saw the red-purple marks again. They reminded him that even though he yearned for her, like a plant for sunlight, or a fish for water, he could not have her, not yet. His fingers, featherlight, traced back up her skin until he could take a hold of her chin.

"Ella," he whispered, "I want you more than I could ever express. I've wanted to touch you like this for so long." His fingers wandered again, starting from the base of her neck and traveling lower over her spine. She curved into his touch and shifted, rubbing against him. He hissed and squeezed her hips to keep her still, eliciting a whimper from her.

He cursed. "We can't, not yet. Not when I want so much from you."

Daniella's shoulders dropped as she looked away, but Greg cupped her face, drawing her gaze back to him. "I'm not rejecting you. Don't you know what you are to me? What you mean to me? You drive me crazy, Daniella." She was so close. So close that if he just leaned in, just an inch, her lips would be against his. He'd swallow her breaths, her moans, her cries as he plunged inside of her … *Fuck.*

Greg shook his head. "One night isn't enough for me. I wouldn't be able to stop myself from making you my mate, and that's not right. It's not fair to you. Not with everything going on."

She cupped his face. "But—"

"I am not a good person, Ella," Greg said sharply.

"Isn't that for me to decide?"

"Do you always have to make sense?"

"You know me well enough to know the answer to that question." She smiled.

He took her in. The way she watched him, how deeply she seemed to want to understand, and her fierce determination to do so. She was so gentle, yet so strong. He finally understood that stepping around the issue would get him nowhere. Greg had promised her honesty, and if she could be open with him, he should do the same for her.

"I am in the middle of a war that you have, unfortunately, been drawn into."

Her eyes widened, and he wrapped his arms around her, bracing her for what he had to say.

"I don't use that word lightly, Ella. This is not the first time, and unless certain people are dealt with, it won't be the last. Zachariah has caused me and my loved ones a lot of pain, and I need you to understand what that means. We don't police in my world, certainly not at this stage. The next time I see that vampire, I am going to kill him with my bare hands."

His gaze shifted downward. "If you can still want me after you know I've done that, then you will have all of me for the rest of our exceptionally long lives. But without that, I can't. It's not fair to ask you to spend forever with me while I hide parts of myself away from you. I know that now."

"Greg," she whispered, but he shook his head and looked away from her. His heart was too exposed. Again, his fingers traced the marks that bastard had left on her. How he wanted to erase them, to replace every fiber of her being with his so that she would never remember that monster.

His voice was gruff as he struggled to push his jealousy and rage aside. "I can heal these for you, if you like."

She cocked her head to the side. "How?"

"I have a healing agent in my blood and saliva."

Daniella stared at him incredulously. "And what would I have to do?"

"Nothing. Just sit here. But try not to squirm around too much. You are still on my lap after all." He tried to lighten the mood with a smile, and while her lips tilted upwards, he could tell she was still irritated with him.

"All right." She lifted her hair, brushing the strands behind her shoulder.

Greg bent towards her hesitantly, giving her time to change her mind. He paused, breathing her in, the soft perfume that still clung to her skin barely noticeable under her own scent—something mild and warm, like apricots and berries drizzled with honey from the sweetest of flowers. He steeled himself.

Stay in control. You don't want to scare her.

He licked her pulse, felt it spike against his tongue. She took a breath as his tongue slid upward, following along each mark that scarred her beautiful maple skin. A whispered moan escaped her lips when he sucked her neck. He couldn't stop himself. Daniella slid her arms around him, burying her hands in his hair. He squeezed her back, tugging her closer until he could feel the rise and fall of her soft breasts pressed so perfectly against his chest.

Her breath caught when he kissed a spot below her ear. He traced the lobe with his tongue and when he nibbled on the flesh, she hissed, a shiver running through her body. She shifted, wrapping her legs around his waist. Her hips circled, then rolled against his own, and Greg's eyes drifted closed as pleasure soared through him. This time, he didn't stop her. Instead, he cupped her ass, urging her to keep moving in such delicious sin.

Daniella gripped at the strands of his hair, panting, moaning with each move. He spread his legs wider, desperately wanting to fit his erection more firmly against her core. He could smell her desire, her wetness, could almost see her swollen lips in his mind's eye, feel her as he slid inside of her.

Greg was frantic now. He tugged her hair just enough to pull her head back, to leave every inch of her throat accessible to him so he could kiss, lick, and suck at her skin. He felt her swallow, the muscles in her throat moving, and it reminded him of her blood, of how it would feel to drink from her. His fangs extended.

Greg pulled his head back, stopping just short of biting her, conflicted. He feared how close he'd come to breaking his promise, and yet he was still so desperate to continue. But when he stared into her eyes, there was no shred of fear. Instead, she met his gaze with wonder and unabashed need.

"Ella?"

She trembled against him and her voice was hushed when she spoke. "I understand what you said and I know why you said it. I know you still want to protect me, to keep me safe. But I've always felt safe with you. Greg … I thought I lost you." Daniella swallowed hard. "I destroyed that room because I thought you were gone. If you have any question about my feelings for you, or what I think about you, remember that."

His eyes widened as her confession squeezed at his heart, making it beat faster.

She rubbed his cheek. "Kiss me, please. It doesn't need to go further. I'll respect your wishes but just … Please, I'm so tired of pretending."

Greg cupped her chin, his finger trailing over her bottom lip. The moment her lips parted and her eyes fluttered closed, he surrendered. He brushed his lips against hers and let out a blissful sigh. He was so damn tired of pretending too, especially when she tasted this good. When her lips were so soft, so warm, so perfect. Again and again he kissed her, trying to be gentle. But then he couldn't take any more. Not of her moans, her hands as they ran over his body, or how she felt against him. He needed more.

Daniella clenched her thighs around his hips as he lifted her and laid her back on the couch, his lips never breaking from her own. She pulled at him when he tried to keep his weight off of her, and finally he gave in, pressing every bit of his body against hers.

Their kiss heated, became wild. He squeezed her back, kneading the plump curves of her ass. Greg licked her lips, nibbled and sucked until her mouth opened. Taking the invitation, he slid his tongue inside and they waged a battle together, one they both won.

Her feet crossed at the base of his back and pushed at his hips. Answering her call, he rocked against her, swallowing her moans, drinking her in. His fingers slipped under her shirt, following the lines of her spine. He circled his hips, pressed against her clit, and she hissed. Greg smiled into the kiss and did it again.

Daniella pulled at him, her hands stroking his skin, squeezing, clawing at his back while they soared higher. When Greg finally lifted his mouth from hers, he felt as if he'd been drugged. He was mindless in his desire for her. Needing to taste her again, he leaned toward her lips, only to be stopped as she placed her fingers against his mouth.

"I promised to respect your wishes," she panted, "but if you touch me like that again, I will make sure you won't stop."

Greg nibbled on her finger. "You're a dangerous woman." He slid his hands out from under her shirt and used their position to roll until he could cradle her beside him.

Daniella's head came to rest under his, while her hand laid right above his racing heart. "I've been called a lot of things in my life, but never dangerous."

"Good," he said darkly. "I like knowing I'm the only person who has seen that side of you."

Her eyebrows shot up. "Was that possessiveness I just heard?"

"Yes." He turned his head towards hers. "If that's okay with you."

"Yes, it is." Her fingertips swirled over his chest as a blush stained her cheeks. "It's a relief to hear you say that. I was worried that you'd want our relationship to stay the way it was, and I don't think I could go back to that, not after tonight."

He captured her hand and brushed his lips against hers. "Neither could I. I'd planned to try and stay away from you. I wanted to give you space, to help you feel comfortable here. But now, when I know I can lie here beside you? I could never give up that chance."

"That makes me really happy to hear." She smiled and her blush deepened. "While today was … difficult, I don't regret it."

He sighed. "I wish things would have happened another way. I never want to see you hurt, and the fact that you were will haunt me for a long time. But I am happy you're here. I'm happy that I've finally gotten to share this part of my life with you." Greg twined his fingers in her hair, his voice deep with emotion as he spoke. "Ella, you are my heart. There is so much more I have to tell you. But please know that I won't rush you. I don't want to ruin the possibility of us growing into more."

She lifted her head to meet his eyes. "Why are you so afraid that something is going to ruin us when I want to be with you? I'm happy with you."

"Because the supernatural world is different. The monsters told in fairytales exist here. My life has afforded me many luxuries. I've visited many places, met incredible people, but the history I've gone through and the current events of today, they're not easy. This world isn't easy, and you deserve better."

Her eyes softened. "I get to decide that, Greg. You care about me so much, and it means the world to me, but I get to decide if I can accept your world. Plus, I believe you're forgetting about the mess I made upstairs. I may be a little late to the game, but I'm still a contender."

He opened his mouth to argue, but upon seeing her glare, he picked the safer option and agreed. "I suppose you have a point."

"Thank you. Now, tell me about vampires. Do you drink blood?"

"Yes," he drawled, taking in her reaction. "I do."

Daniella raised an eyebrow. "Human blood?"

"Yes, typically, although sometimes animal blood."

She frowned. "But I've seen you eat normal food. Does it provide nourishment to you, or do you just eat it for appearances?"

"I enjoy normal food. I can still taste it and eat it, but it doesn't replace the nourishment blood provides. There are some exceptions to that though, such as a raw steak, but it's the difference between eating a snack or a meal."

"What is it like? Does it have a taste? Do you have a favorite kind?"

Greg chuckled at her curiosity. He loved to see her mind work, the joy in her gaze as puzzle pieces fit to paint a picture. "All blood tastes different. Different blood types have different nutrients. I suppose I don't have a favorite." His eyes drifted down to her neck. *Yet.*

"So, you … take blood from people? You bite them often, I mean?"

He chuckled. "No, I haven't drunk blood from any living being since we established blood banks. And I only need to drink blood every one to two weeks."

"Vampires established blood banks? I guess that makes sense." Daniella laughed, and then a soft blush tinged her cheeks. She bit her lip, drawing his gaze "Do you want to drink my blood?"

His humor left him with her question. Greg ran the back of his hand over her cheek as he whispered, "I do."

Her eyes widened, but she didn't pull away from him.

"Taking someone's blood can be a sexual experience. And when a vampire finds his mate, it's required to cement the bond." He stroked her cheek with his thumb, scared she may fear him now. "It doesn't hurt. I would never, ever hurt you or do anything without your consent. Please don't let that thought scare you. I don't want you to be afraid of me."

Daniella leaned into his touch. She cupped his palm against her skin and nuzzled it. "I'm not scared of you, Greg." She kissed his hand. "I know you would never hurt me. I trust you."

"You're taking this all very well."

Her gaze turned mischievous. "I just keep remembering everyone has their kinks. Who am I to judge?"

A bark of laughter escaped him. “That’s true, although”—his voice deepened as his hand slipped down the back of her neck, pulling her to him—“I’m curious what yours are.”

She smiled as her lips neared his own. “If you treat me right, I’ll tell you.”

Greg flipped her onto her back, fitting his body against hers once more. Daniella gasped at the sudden change but wound her arms around him as he kissed her temple, her cheek, his lips brushing against her skin with every word. “I will treat you like the goddess that you are. Like the core of my universe. I will give you anything you want, every part of me, just for this.”

And then he kissed her as if he were starving for her taste, because he was. He would never get enough of her. His body exploded and he drank her in. Every whimper, every moan, every caress pulled him under, until the world around him completely disappeared and all that was left was her.

10

Daniella was nervous. Even the fresh cool breeze hitting her face and the scent of the sea as they drove along the coast couldn't fully erase her worries.

They were on their way to meet Astrid, an immortal who specialized in understanding and assisting with abilities. While it was true that what she had experienced last night was otherworldly, Daniella had done her best to remind herself that this was her new reality, and nothing could change that fact. But she'd heard the voices again, like an internal alerting system that buzzed when she needed guidance, and even though they were helpful—caring even—they reminded her of her mother's demise.

Yes, she wanted help to manage her new abilities, but what if there was more to all of this? What if something was actually wrong with her mentally? What if she was having some sort of psychotic break? What if—

As if sensing her thoughts, Greg reached over and squeezed her hand. "It's going to be okay, I promise. You don't need to be nervous."

"Am I that transparent?"

"To me you are." He kissed her hand, bringing a small smile to her lips. "Astrid is a good person. I've known her for a very long time and she's helped many of my people. I know all of this has happened pretty quickly and, while you're handling it exceptionally well, it has been a huge shock. But think of this as a chance for answers. She'll be able to help you and give you some peace of mind."

Daniella rubbed the back of his hand as she took a deep breath. "Okay."

It took another half an hour before Greg came to a stop down a narrow brick road lined with oak trees and cottage-style shops. Astrid's storefront was picturesque. Its bright sky-blue exterior, sandwiched between cedar paneling and flower boxes, made Daniella smile. It was nothing like the tall skyscrapers of New York City. She liked it immediately.

Greg opened the door for her, and the first thing she noticed was the smell—fragrant but mild spices that paired well with the fresh scents of wood, citrus, and pine. Dried lemon and orange slices hung from the window with chimes, along with drying herbs. She knew one of them was rosemary, and another looked like lavender, but she couldn't identify the rest.

The shop was covered with crystals, cards, and books, so many that she couldn't count them all. It should have been overwhelming, yet the space felt welcoming, serene. She'd gone into occult shops before, but never one so peaceful.

A curtain moved in the distance, revealing a beautiful ebony woman. Her black curls reached past her shoulders and down her waist, contrasting with her silver eyes that seemed to swirl. She was ethereal, beautiful.

"Ancient", the voices whispered in her mind.

The woman smiled at her, the greeting warm and genuine. But when her gaze settled on Greg, she laughed. "Greg! It's been too long." Moving forward with silent steps, she gave him a tight hug.

He returned the embrace. "Hey, Astrid. Thank you for seeing us on such short notice."

"Of course!" Astrid patted his back.

It warmed Daniella's heart to see the exchange. Knowing Greg had friends, people he could rely on in between the multitude of the responsibilities he'd shared with her last night, made her hopes rise. Perhaps these people had helped to ease his loneliness.

"And you're his mate!" Astrid pulled Daniella in for a hug. "I'm so happy to finally meet you! This has been a long time coming."

A nervous laugh escaped Daniella's lips. She wasn't sure how this woman knew their situation, but she answered honestly. "Yes, it has."

She caught Greg's jubilant smile over Astrid's shoulder.

The woman chuckled. "I like her, she's got spirit. Come on back. Greg tells me you need a little guidance with your gifts."

Daniella followed after her with Greg in tow. "Thank you, I'm not sure how to deal with them."

Astrid closed the curtain behind them and motioned for them to sit down at a table. "Now that's not true. They may seem new to you now, but you've always had them. You've just forgotten how they work is all. Give me your hand."

Daniella hesitated, but placed her hand in Astrid's. She clasped their hands together, her hold strong but gentle.

"Every person on this planet has an ability," Astrid began. "Painting is an ability; singing is an ability. Humans have just backpedaled to only understand and believe in things they can see and study. They've forgotten the old magic that exists around them. But you, I, and even Greg can access that. Magic is in you, always has been and always will be."

Daniella jumped as a book moved, flying from behind her and coming to a stop beside Astrid. The pages turned of their own accord.

"I'm sorry, I didn't mean to scare you," Astrid said.

Daniella looked from the book, to Astrid, and back. *Flying books. It's just a flying book. This is the life you have to get used to. With everything you've done, this should seem like child's play.* She took a steadying breath. "No, it's okay. How did you do that?"

"My ability is to connect to things by threads. Have you ever heard the saying 'cutting ties with someone'?"

Daniella nodded.

"It comes from old magic. My ability is to create threads and use them for things I need. Anything I touch or come in contact with creates a thread, and when I need something, such as a book"—Astrid waved a hand and the book spun—"or to read another person's ability, I use that thread to do so."

"But doesn't that get tiring after a while? I don't know a lot about the occult or magic, but I thought you cut ties to keep people from bringing your energy down."

Astrid smiled. "It can, and it will if I'm not careful, but I take care to protect myself. Think of it like a type of residue. By touching your hands, I've left a little on you which I can use to create my thread. When I'm done, I'll remove it. If you want it to stay, then it will."

Daniella stared at the book and then at the impressive, eccentric woman in front of her. "That's incredible."

She laughed. "If you think that's amazing, wait until you see what you can do."

Daniella gasped. "You already know?"

"Mhmm, but I like to learn the history of things. It makes sharing the knowledge with you easier. When was the first time something seemed different? I get the idea that you went searching for answers."

Greg, who so far had been silently leaning against a wall, moved behind her. He rested his hand on her shoulder, giving it a small squeeze, lending her his strength.

"My intuition has always been strong. But I'm beginning to think that's not really what I thought it was. I know when bad things are going to happen. Not what, but sometimes where. It feels … dark, and heavy. Sometimes I can ignore it if something is just going to inconvenience me, like being a few minutes late to work or an event. But other times, like yesterday, it makes me sick."

She looked up at Greg for a moment, and at his nod she continued. "Everywhere I went, I felt sick. I couldn't figure out why, and then I was attacked when I got home."

Astrid's eyes widened and her gaze shifted to Greg's.

"It was Zachariah," Greg bit out.

"That bastard." Astrid crossed her arms. "I should have castrated him when I had the chance."

Daniella choked back a laugh at her outburst.

"He pisses me off. Sorry, continue."

"No, it's okay. I'm right there with you. After Greg got there, I became overwhelmed. I just felt this deep rage build inside of me, and then I electrocuted him."

At Astrid's raised eyebrow, Greg chuckled. "Don't get excited. He survived."

She pouted. "We'll have to work on that. Anything else?"

"I also destroyed a room in Greg's house. I was having an anxiety attack and needed to breathe. Then Greg's window shattered and vines poured into the room. And I've started hearing these voices—"

"Voices?" Greg asked.

Daniella fidgeted under his stare. "Yes. I wasn't sure how to tell you. It started last night. I only hear them sometimes, normally when I'm around you."

"Interesting." Astrid sat forward. "What do they say?"

Daniella's gaze flickered back up to Greg's. "Well, whenever you're struggling with telling me something, or hiding something from me, the voices tell me what you're going through. It's almost like they're trying to help me understand you or reach you somehow." She shook her head with a sigh. "It's difficult to explain."

"And what do they feel like?"

She paused. The question should have been strange, but Astrid was right. They had a feeling. "Each one is different," Daniella said. "Some are more grounded, others more violent, but they are all ancient. When I hear them, it feels like speaking with something that has more knowledge than I do, and in turn it makes me feel as though I have to respect them. At first, they were external, to the point that I thought you could hear them." She motioned to Greg. "But then I realized you couldn't. Now they've become more internal, like this knowing feeling inside of me. Does that make any sense?"

"It does."

The book beside Astrid moved, laying on its spine in front of Daniella. She hesitated to touch the enchanted object, and so Astrid leaned forward and tapped on a paragraph. "Your abilities are elemental."

Daniella read over the short blurb about people who could communicate with the elements and call on them to use their powers. It seemed impossible. "But that doesn't make sense. All I've ever felt is darkness, and how would the voices come into play?"

"When most people think of something dark, they become afraid. Monsters under the bed and all that nonsense." Astrid waved her hand dismissively. "Because of that personification, what you were feeling was the being of darkness. It was warning you of someone's intent to harm you. As you became more connected to it, I'm sure that expanded to any general negativity or minor annoyance. The other voices are attached to other beings. As for you"—she pointed to Greg—"because you were hiding something from her, they revealed it."

Greg chuckled nervously. "I'm not sure how it feels to know I'm being spied on."

Daniella shrugged, a small smile teasing her lips. "Don't blame me. I'm just a conduit." Her attention shifted back to Astrid. "Why do you think they're talking to me now?"

"Did your parents ever teach you anything, any odd phrases?"

The mood of the room changed immediately. Greg went to speak for her, but she stopped him with a squeeze of his hand "I don't know my father, and my mother died when I was a child."

"I'm so sorry to hear that." Astrid reached across the table and squeezed her other hand.

Daniella couldn't tell if it was the shop, Astrid's abilities, or her own, but she could feel the comfort, sincerity, and strength radiating from both Astrid and Greg so strongly it brought tears to her eyes.

Greg bent down beside her and wiped one tear as it escaped. "Baby—"

She shook her head, wiping her eyes. "It's okay. I could feel both of you. Your compassion was so strong it was … breathtaking. Thank you both for that. I'm sorry for worrying you, but I promise I'm okay."

Greg sighed and nodded as she turned back to Astrid.

"To answer your question, I don't remember much about her, but she had some odd phrases and a habit of talking out loud to voices. When I was a child, I would ask her what she was doing and she always said she was talking to her friends. Most people just thought she was crazy."

There was a somber look in Astrid's eyes when she responded, and Daniella wondered if she had experienced the same cruelty. "It sounds like she had the same ability as you, just not developed. Long ago, beings reigned all over this land. Some of them were real, and some of them were created by humans who worshipped them. Take fire, for instance. That was the best discovery to man at the time because it was something new, so they worshipped it. When their crops were dying, they worshipped rain. When their plants were fertilized, they worshipped the earth to keep them healthy. While those beings may have come from others, they eventually took on a whole life of their own and grew into their own power.

"Much like I can create threads, they can be called upon. When witches in movies and shows 'call the corners', they're communicating to the beings in those elements. You can do the same thing, just without all the hoo-ha. Here."

The book lifted, shut, and went back onto a bookshelf behind Daniella, who tried not to jump.

"Close your eyes and try to create something."

Daniella's eyes darted around the room and the various objects and items that Astrid clearly treasured. "I don't know if that's a good idea. I don't want to break anything in your shop."

"You won't." Astrid smiled. "You did that because you were scared. Are you scared right now?"

"I'm hesitant, but no, I'm not scared."

"Good. Being nervous can be a positive type of energy. It means you're willing to embrace possibility. Now, close your eyes."

Daniella did so, taking a deep breath to calm herself.

"Now think of something you wish you had in front of you, something from an element. Earth, fire, water, air, light, dark, it doesn't matter which, just pick one and then visualize it coming to you."

There was still a bit of fear deep within her. With each breath, she tried to work through it, knowing she would need to calm her doubt to focus properly. Then it dawned on her that wasn't what she needed. If darkness was what she was used to, maybe what she needed the most right now was peace. With that idea in mind, she tried to think of how to bring it to fruition. Did she just call on a being? Speak to them? Daniella gave herself a mental shake. When she'd attacked Zachariah, or needed to breathe, she didn't vocalize the need to anyone but herself. It was instinctual, and perhaps that need, the ultimate desire for something, was how she communicated.

What does peace look like to you? What makes you calm?

Daniella took another deep breath.

Air.

A vibration started within her as she focused. She searched for air, for fresh, clean air. A window unlatched, letting a breeze into the room. But she wanted more. She wanted a connection, a physical touch to the earth around her.

A thin vine wrapped around her wrist, making her eyes snap open. It grew, swirling over her skin. A bud erupted, revealing an iris, and then another and another. They slid between her hands, crossing and spreading up her arms until she laughed from the joy of it all.

When she lifted her head, the lights in the shop glowed yellow and she knew it was for her. She settled back in the chair and smiled in childish delight.

Astrid squeezed her hands. "See? There's nothing for you to be afraid of. You and the beings are connected, and as long as you keep your head straight, there's nothing you can't do."

Daniella's euphoria continued, leaving her with an extra bounce in her step. After saying goodbye to Astrid, Greg draped his arm around her shoulders as they walked side by side. They talked briefly, spending most of the time enjoying the beautiful weather, neighboring shops, and each other's company.

He took her to get ice cream, where she got a cookie dough and cream concoction and he a sea salt caramel pecan flavor. She decided later, when their mouths and bodies were crushed together in a heated kiss behind the store, that the flavor tasted much better when combined with his lips. Today was good. Today felt right. Being with him felt right, and nothing could take her down from that cloud.

Daniella had been so focused on her time with him, on being there and present in this space, that she hadn't felt it. She hadn't realized the darkness was back—hard, cold, and spreading through her body—until they pulled into the driveway of Greg's house and parked beside two other vehicles.

"Greg," she forced through labored breaths, "something's wrong."

He took one look at her, followed her line of sight, and leapt from the car. She tailed behind him, not able to keep up with his vampiric speed. When she caught up to him, he was in the foyer with Luke and Mya. These were her friends, people she loved and cared about. Normally she would have embraced them, laughed, and felt love at their nearness, but their expressions were too sad.

Greg turned toward her. "Ella…" He trailed off, his skin pale.

"What is it? What happened?" When no one spoke, the ball of panic in her chest squeezed her heart in an iron grip. Shaking, she yelled, "Just tell me!"

Luke glanced at Mya, who sighed. Mya took a sheet of newspaper from him and handed it to her. "I'm sorry," she said.

Daniella's gaze shifted from hers to the page in her hand, scanning the title "Animal Attack Leaves Woman Dead". Confused, she read on, then stopped, her eyes moving to a small picture of a beautiful blonde woman. A familiar blonde woman. Her eyes moved between the picture and the article, taking in more information, the words ricocheting around her mind. *Ripped throat, bloody, teeth marks, teeth.* And then she saw the name.

Daniella broke. She shattered because she knew. She screamed, setting the page on fire because she knew. It was Stacy, and she was dead.

11

Daniella struggled to open her eyes. The lids were glued shut, puffy and swollen from the tears she'd shed a few short hours ago. Greg had done everything he could for her. He'd brought her upstairs to his bedroom and held her until she'd cried herself to the point of exhaustion. He'd run his fingers through her hair, telling her it wasn't her fault and apologizing for her pain over and over. Then he'd just hummed to her while she wallowed in her grief.

The room felt cold without his presence, darker than normal. She searched through the emptiness as if it would give her answers. Then she remembered the last time she had seen Stacy and how the darkness had reacted to her touch. The way it had morphed into something ugly and horrid under Daniella's skin, like daggers piercing her heart. She had simply dismissed it as a fluke, because at the time, Stacy didn't fit. She shouldn't have fit in this world of chaos and darkness, but now she did, and that was on her. Stacy's death was on her.

If Daniella had known more, she could have warned her. If she would have listened harder or believed, if she would have been more focused, maybe things would be different. But none of that mattered now. Stacy was gone, a young woman taken long before her time.

Daniella came to the obvious conclusion that Zachariah had killed her. Everyone who knew of her friendship with Stacy was on the first floor of this house, and none of them would have ever hurt Stacy or her. Questions swarmed in her mind. If she had gone with Zachariah, would Stacy still be alive right now? Was he planning on killing her just for sport, or did he kill her because he couldn't get Daniella? Was this just another way to hurt her? Was this how he taught her that he was still in control, that he could get to her at any place, at any time, and would keep going until he got what he wanted?

"Stop! Enough!" the voices shouted, but the damage had been done.

Energy swarmed within her, powered by her rage. She glided towards the balcony, forcing the doors open without moving a finger. As she neared the railing, she looked down, needing to feel the earth at her feet. There was no room for doubt or fear as Daniella used the air to float over the railing and down to the ground. She had split herself away from reality, from the human constructs of what was possible and impossible. Instead, there was only need, the ultimate desire to shake the earth, to unleash her wrath. The air howled, crashing around her like the wild sea. Distant shouting came from behind her, but the words were sucked into the void she'd crafted. She couldn't hear them now, and she didn't care to. Her fury was all-consuming.

Raising her hands outward, Daniella called the clouds to her as the wind grew harsher, wilder. It whipped around her and she called for more. Turning her gaze upward, she gathered energy and felt renewed in her vengeance when lightning flashed. One bolt, two bolts, three, the sky turning a violent white-blue at every spark. As the rain cascaded from the sky, frozen balls of ice followed. Large hailstones cracked against tree branches, snapping their stems from the force.

Strong arms wrapped around her. Greg held her, shouting that it would be okay, that she had to stop. But she didn't. She couldn't stop, not now.

Greg turned her roughly but paused at the fresh tears falling down her face.

"It's all my fault! He killed her because of me," she cried through the storm she'd created.

He didn't respond. Instead, he gathered her in his embrace. Daniella twined her arms around him, clutching his shirt as she buried herself in his chest.

The lightning stopped and the wind ceased to scream, but the rain continued to fall over its mistress, mixing with her tears.

After taking a shower, Daniella put on the clothes Mya pulled out for her. While she was grateful for her care, it didn't ease the bitterness that had settled within her. She held the feeling around her like a protective shield. This wasn't the end of her journey or her fight. There was still the embezzlement, a war, her powers, her feelings for Greg, this family, immortals. There was too much, and she couldn't slow down, not yet. She had to keep going, and if that were the case, she would do so by turning every bit of pain she felt into a weapon.

Daniella walked into the study to see Greg dressed in his business attire. Her heart skipped a beat when he focused on her, and then she took in the sadness in his eyes. "What happened?" she asked.

"Nothing. The council has summoned me for an emergency meeting and I'll need to go into the office. I'm sorry." His voice was full of remorse. "I don't want to leave you."

She breathed a sigh of relief. "No, that's okay. I've taken up enough of your time over the last few days."

The flash in his eyes was her only warning as he stormed toward her. She gasped, but before she could retreat, he pulled her toward him and crashed his lips against hers. For a moment, she hesitated, and then fell vulnerable to his touch, his taste. Her arms wrapped around his neck as he devoured her. He took all that she was and gave just as much of himself back.

At the clearing of a throat, they broke apart from the kiss.

"I'll wait for you by the cars," Luke said, grinning like a complete and utter idiot.

Her cheeks warmed as Greg nodded. At Luke's fading steps, she smoothed the small wrinkle in his jacket. "You should get going."

He ran his finger under her chin, forcing her to meet his gaze. "Not until I address what you just said. You could never take up too much of my time because you are worth every second of every day. Eternity is not long enough for me to spend with you. It does not even compare to how long I want to be with you. Nothing expresses the amount of joy and happiness you bring me, or the depths of my emotions for you, but you are worth them." He brushed a strand of hair behind her ear. "You are worth everything, Daniella."

"Greg," she stuttered, drowning in the mess he'd made of her heart, "I-I don't think—"

"I know you don't. I know why, and I will prove that you should not feel guilty for your existence. You have positively affected so many more lives than you know. You have been my strength without even realizing it. Don't forget that, Ella. Don't forget the lives you affect, the good you've done and still have left to do. Don't forget what you mean to the people around you, those that love you."

He kissed her again, bursting her fragile heart open under the spell he'd woven. She clung to him and the light he gave her in the face of her despair.

"Mya's going to stay here with you. But when I'm done with the meeting, I'll pick us up dinner and then we'll talk, okay?"

"Okay."

He kissed her cheek before finally slipping out of their embrace, and she held onto the words he'd left her to keep her sane.

12

When Daniella first met Mya, she'd reminded her of a wolf: big, fluffy, and able to bite your head off in less than ten seconds. But after she'd gotten to know her, she understood it was just an outer layer. Daniella had always suspected Mya used it to protect herself, although she'd never quite figured out why. Now it made more sense.

Mya had made it through periods of times where women were believed to be worthless, where they needed to dress and behave in ways that modern women found demeaning. Daniella had a new-found respect for Mya and her strength. That strength was admirable, and an inspiration for what she desperately needed to maintain, a semblance of balance right now to keep her grief at bay.

"On a scale of one to ten, how mad are you at me?" Mya called out before Daniella entered the kitchen.

She thought for a moment while taking a seat beside Mya. "Around a two."

"Huh, I would have assumed at least a six."

"No. One, because I know if anyone hated keeping me in the dark, it would be you. You don't have patience to deal with stupidity, much less lying. Two, because it's rare for you to be apologetic. I barely made Greg or Luke grovel for the transgression. You wouldn't bother."

Mya tapped her fingers on the table. "Well, you're not wrong there, but I am sorry. I never wanted to hurt you. You're like a sister to me, and I adore you."

Daniella smiled. "Same here." She nodded towards the laptop as automated numbers moved on the screen. "Is that about the embezzlement?"

Mya sighed, fussing with a dark brown strand that had fallen from her high bun. "I still have a lot to investigate. For some reason, the answer to all of this is eluding me, and it's pissing me off."

"I should have asked Greg to bring my laptop from the office. I also don't know where my purse or cell phone are. Could I borrow yours to text him?"

"Don't worry about that. Greg had me look at your phone to see if it could be tracked, which it could. He's getting you a new one and a card tied to his account while he's in NYC."

Her eyes widened. "Wait, what?"

Mya smirked. "The man's got it bad, and from the looks of it, so do you. Word of advice: don't say anything stupid like he doesn't need to do this, or shouldn't do this, yada yada. Just accept it. It's easier that way."

Daniella opened her mouth to respond but couldn't form any words. A blush spread across her cheeks as she tried to hide her shy smile. Greg's kindness and the strength of his feelings warmed her heart. He made all of those wishes and fantasies that she'd kept at bay for so long seem not only attainable, but actively reciprocated.

The computer chimed and Mya cursed, hitting the table with a sigh.

"Can I help somehow?"

Mya studied her for a moment. "How much do you know?"

"What do you mean?" Daniella cocked her head to the side.

"I mean, what do you think happened at the office?"

Her brow furrowed in confusion. "Well, I found out about the embezzlement at the same time you guys did. Greg initially told me he wanted me to stay out of the office for a few weeks on a fake vacation because he thought the theft was being pointed at me. I now know that's not one hundred percent true. I know Zachariah was the one who did it, but he had to have inside help. He wouldn't have been able to commit the crime otherwise."

Mya raised an eyebrow. "Why?"

Daniella sighed, shoving her fingers through her hair. "Because he may have been at my apartment."

Mya whistled. "Sleeping with the enemy? Damn girl."

"Please don't tease me about it. Alcohol led to very poor decisions that night."

"A vampire booty call. I'd be proud of you if it were anyone else."

Daniella elbowed her. "Hush. It was not one of my finer moments."

Mya typed rapidly now. "Do you know what time he arrived and what time he left?"

"Somewhere around 1:30 a.m., and he left a few minutes after sunrise."

"Hmm. So he killed them first and then triggered the security alert."

Daniella drew back. "Killed them? Killed who? What are you talking about?"

Mya muttered a curse under her breath and faced her. "Fuck, Dani, when you said crime, I thought…" She sighed. "Zachariah didn't just steal money from the company. He killed twenty-two vampires before he did it."

"Oh God. Oh God, I think I'm going to be sick."

"Shit—"

Daniella barely made it to the trash can before vomiting. Mya held back her hair as she heaved. When Daniella became more stable, Mya brought her a glass of water.

"Thank you."

"It's okay. I'm sorry. I should have let Greg tell you. He would have," Mya insisted as she led Daniella to the bar stool.

"No, it's okay. I'm close with each of you, and I want you all to fill me in if I don't know something." She stroked the glass with her thumb. "I know Greg would have told me, but we just haven't had a lot of time. Every day something else happens." Her eyes slid to Mya. "Has it always been this way?"

Mya shook her head. "No. Things were good and had been good for a while. There were some terrible times, of course, and sometimes I don't know how we made it through, but we did. The war picked back up about a century ago. Each time, it's someone new. Someone always thinks that we shouldn't live beside humans, that our proper place is to reign over them. It's always a new vampire, one that doesn't understand what we've gone through and seen. That even though we are stronger, there are simply more humans."

Mya rested her head in her palm and shrugged. "It's not about conquering or being the top predator. It's about creating a peaceful co-existence. Whenever vampires appear with those ideals, we shut them down. But Zachariah? I don't know. He doesn't even seem smart enough to do all of this, but every time we think we'll catch him, he slips through our fingers." She rubbed her temples. "He's caused more carnage and erased more of our history than anyone else."

Daniella shook her head. Her voice wavered as she spoke. "So much pain, so much death … I'm beginning to understand why you all kept this from me."

Her thoughts turned to Stacy. Stacy wasn't a vampire. She shouldn't have been dragged into this mess, but she was. And the others. How many people had died in these useless battles, especially over the course of a century?

She didn't realize she was shaking until Mya squeezed her shoulder. "What about the lives of the vampires who were killed?"

"We have something of a cleanup crew. They tidy up any loose ends. Any work that needs to be done, investigations, housing payments, moving furniture, pets, they handle all of that. Dominick and Merida review their work to make sure nothing was missed and provide a final report to Greg."

"But what about family?" Her voice rose. "Don't vampires have families?"

Mya sighed. "When they become part of our circle, they leave all of that behind, Dani. They have to, for the same reasons you're seeing now."

A pained expression flashed in Mya's eyes, but she continued. "We take care of our own, but that doesn't mean there aren't casualties, and to keep everyone safe, only immediate family is brought in. Greg meets with each victim's family. If a vampire had a mate, we will take care of them, make sure they're kept afloat, and watch out for them. It's the same if they had children. Some vampires have extended family, grandchildren, or great-grandchildren who were born long after they became a vampire. For their protection, the vampire has to stay away. They may send anonymous presents or donations, set up funds for their education or life, which the cleaners make sure continue, but otherwise they have to keep that life separate from their vampiric one. No visitations, sharing anything traceable, and so on."

Mya grimaced. "It's not an easy life, but any vampire that comes into any circle agrees to those terms before they do. It may sound cruel, but—"

"It's not cruel. It's lonely." Daniella lifted her gaze from the counter and the look in her eyes made Mya draw back. "How do you kill a vampire?"

"That's not something you need to worry about."

"But it is. All of this is because of one vampire. I understand others may follow his ideals, but he's the one killing people right now, and it affects everyone. I mean, didn't you stay behind just to protect me?"

Mya's eyes narrowed. "It's not the only reason I'm here."

Daniella glared back at her. "Fine, but it's still one of the reasons. I need to learn how to take care of myself. Teach me how. Neither Greg nor Luke would ever show me, and even if they did, they'd go easy on me. You won't. Greg will be out for a while, so we have plenty of time."

Mya sighed and tapped her fingers on the counter again.

"Please?"

"You have a point, and it would be good for you to know how to defend yourself. But I have to be straight with you." She shrugged. "I have two abilities. One is to heal. Greg and Luke have a fraction of it because I shared it with them, but it's only a fraction. Even if you get a hit in, and that's a *big* if, it's not going to slow me down enough to stop me from countering. The second is speed. I'm fast. You aren't going to be able to keep up with me, end of story."

"You're also ruthless, competitive, and clearly not humble," Daniella said with a grunt.

Mya smiled and raised her hands in mock agreement. "I call it how I see it. But my point is, the you sitting next to me right now is not ready for this at all. If we're going to do this, I need your complete focus, and right now it's elsewhere. So, go deal with your friend's death, however you need to. Pain will get you far. It will motivate you, it will give you strength when you think all of yours has faded, but it will also eat away at you until you are nothing but a vast dark hole that crumbles under its own weight. If you need to scream, scream. If you need to throw a tree, cause a tornado or whatever that was earlier, then do it. Just don't wreck the house."

The ground was damp under her feet. The puddle she'd stepped into splashed back at her, but she paid it no mind. Daniella's thoughts had faded to a whisper. There were no voices, no darkness, no emotions, just a pull.

An invisible string that connected her to somewhere she knew intimately, and so she let it lead her.

Three days ago, she would have been scared, concerned about her irrational childish behavior. She loved the woods, loved nature, but she never had time for it, much less embraced it like she did now. She would have wondered where she was going, if she knew how to get back, thought of meetings she might be late for if she couldn't, set numerous alarms, and turned on the location on her phone to make sure she would be safe. Those were all things she had to do in NYC.

There was a certain necessary control required when navigating the bustling streets. It's how one avoided collision, a spilled drink, assault, or stolen property. It was how she kept herself out of danger. Keeping a tight, level head was how she made it through, combined with constant momentum, moving one foot in front of the other until she reached her destination. That had always been her belief, but now she realized her life never had to be that way.

The earth had freedom, something she never knew she needed. Yet here, surrounded by the forest, the scents of pine, maple, and even the poison ivy, she realized this was where she belonged. She knew it would take care of her, that it would keep her safe, as long as she relinquished control, as long as she listened.

Daniella went deeper into the lush forest until she found a break in the trees. Rocks jutted in a circle, irregular yet smooth. They surrounded a bed of wildflowers. Weeds to other people—tiny, insignificant things that would have been plucked from the earth for their unsightliness. They now felt like her greatest treasures.

Careful not to step on them, she wove through the rows before coming to stand in the center. Lifting her head up to the sky, she breathed in and basked in the sunlight, letting it warm her. Then she sank to her knees and cried. She cried for Stacy, for the lost vampires. She cried for Greg, Luke, and Mya, for the torture and turmoil they had experienced. She cried for their responsibilities, the weight on Greg's shoulders.

She cried for herself, for never knowing she could be this version of herself that craved so much more but expected so much less. For the toxic ways she had lived her life, the busyness she no longer craved, the distractions, the peace she compromised, the abilities that had hidden within her for such a long time. Had she always lived this way, as half of a person, fearing that if she let go even for a moment, she would turn to drugs like her mother?

She cried for who her mother had been during her good times, who she had been during her bad, and who she could have been with guidance, with someone like Greg in her life. Someone who could sympathize and guide her abilities. Someone who had just listened.

A part of her wished that could have been her, but she was only a child back then. That was far too great of an ask, but now it became a driving force. In three days, her life had completely flipped on its head. She had these abilities, this knowledge, these people, this life, and she realized they were all things she wanted. All things she needed.

Daniella brushed her hands on her knees, wiping off the dirt, and swiped at her eyes with the inside of her shirt. Weaving her hands through the flowers she'd crushed, she spoke softly.

"Maybe I'm crazy for trying this or saying it out loud, but I don't care anymore." The world seemed to hump as she spoke. "Spirit of darkness, whatever, whoever you are, I don't know if you are connected with death, or if you can carry this message there, but if you can, please, wherever Stacy is, let her know I'm sorry. I'm sorry she died. I'm sorry for whatever role I played in her death. I know I'm not to blame. I know things happen for a reason, but I also know she was targeted because of me. I loved her." She sniffled. "I still love her. I can still picture her smile, I can still hear her violin, I can still think of all the times she worried about me. She was a great friend, and if she's somewhere out there, please let her know that. I'm going to do better. I'm going to finally listen, to take time for myself. I'm going to stop pushing so incredibly hard to just be okay, to be this person I think I'm supposed to be because I shouldn't need anyone." She released a shaky breath. "I'm going to let go of this idea that if I'm not in control, I won't know what to do."

A sad laugh escaped her. "Clearly, I haven't known what to do for most of my life, but I want to learn."

More tears rolled down her cheeks as she trembled. "Let her know that, please, and please, you, the others, the spirits in the elements, help me. I don't want to be half of myself anymore. I don't want to be blind to these abilities or this world anymore. I just want to be whole. I want to be happy instead of temporarily existing and being content with that. I can't go back to my old life, where all my plants are in pots and I live in a polluted and overpopulated city. Where I can't see the tops of mountains or breathe in clean fresh air. I can't be diluted. This world, this place where vampires exist, where I have abilities, where I can figure out who I want to be, not who I think I need to be, is the world I'm meant to live in. I want to learn to have faith in that. I want to learn to have faith in this." She brushed the flowers in her hands. "So please, help me."

The flowers grew, their stems sprouting and rising higher and higher until they reached her chest. It delighted her so much that she laughed, the sound mixing with a new stream of tears.

Daniella made her way back to the house when she was done and paused when she saw Mya waiting for her outside.

A knowing smile touched her lips, and Mya adjusted her hair in its bun. "Better?"

"Yeah." Daniella stretched her arms outwards and then up, rolling her shoulders back. "Are you going to teach me how to fight now?"

"Yep, but when I whoop your ass, don't say I didn't warn you."

13

All Greg wanted was to get back home to Daniella. He'd always hated being away from her, but never more than now, when she was in so much pain and distress. She needed someone to comfort her, and he wanted to be that person. But instead, he was stuck here.

The council meeting had taken almost four hours, much longer than he had initially expected. All because of Zachariah's bullshit. While many of the council members held Greg in high regard, they weren't known for their patience or sympathy. Some members went as far as to state that the vampires Greg lost were a sign of his weakened power and authority. He knew what they were up to. They just wanted his territory and were willing to use any means to get it, even unsubstantiated rumors. Fuckers.

Fear and greed were nasty emotions, but together they were destructive. If he wasn't careful, everything that he built and everyone he protected would end up torn apart. But he wouldn't worry about that now. The future was tomorrow's problem; the present was today's, and he had more than enough issues here.

That Stacy's death had been publicized was a huge issue for their world. This had not been the first time Zachariah—or another otherworldly creature—had taken the life of a human, but they were trained to keep these things hidden from the normal world. As long as Greg kept that from happening again and dealt with Zachariah within the next year, he would be fine. And he would get him sooner rather than later.

It was clear Zachariah had set his sights on Daniella, and the knowledge made Greg's blood boil. He would come after her again, and the moment he did, Greg would delight in ripping his spine out of his body. Then the war would be over.

His muscles rippled under his shirt, veins squeezed and tensed as rage rushed through him. He needed a distraction, to either to let his powers flow through him, or to feed. But he couldn't here or at home, not in the way he needed. He didn't want to scare Daniella. But he was teetering on the edge. There had been too much, too soon, too fast: the events, his guilt, the racing of his mind, Daniella's pain, and the deep desire to mate with her, to make her his *forever*. His fist clenched. He was losing focus.

Greg forced himself to relax a moment before the door opened and a tiny bundle of brown curls awkwardly ran towards him.

"GG!"

He laughed, picked Iris up in his arms, and gave her a tight hug. "Hello, angel!" He looked at Dominick, still chuckling. "I didn't know she was coming here today."

Dominick smiled and took a seat in a nearby chair. "We're taking her out of day care for a few days. With everything going on, she's safer with us."

Greg nodded and pushed through the tightening in his heart at the thought of his goddaughter being hurt. He tickled her as a distraction. With a kiss on top of her head, he sat her on his lap. He turned to speak to her father but stopped when her tiny fists pounded on his chest.

"GG!" she demanded.

"Yes, sweetie?"

Iris tried to stand and Greg held her under her arms to keep her steady. She grabbed his face with her tiny hands and stared right into his soul. "Why sad?"

He blinked, wide-eyed. Iris' ability as a born vampire was to see the emotions of others, but he hadn't realized they'd gotten that strong. He smoothed his hand over her head. "I'm okay, sweetie."

She twisted her lips and stomped her foot on his knee. "Stop sad!" she demanded, then gave him a hug and squirmed until he guided her to the ground.

"Did I just get told off by a two-year-old?"

"Yep." Dom picked up his daughter and tapped her on the nose before turning his gaze on Greg. "What's up, boss?"

"There's just been a lot going on and it's getting to me this time, that's all."

Dom raised an eyebrow. "I don't think I've ever heard you say the pressure was getting to you. Nice to see that even though you're old, you're not set in your ways. Growth is good, my friend."

Greg glared at him. "I get no respect around here."

"Was never a part of the deal. Now, what's going on?"

Greg used his ability to pick up several paper clips and a pack of Post-it notes, floating them around Iris in a circle. Each time Iris tried to grasp one of the flying objects, Greg would pull it away from her. Again and again she tried, until she jumped off of her father's lap to chase them around the room.

"There's more at stake this time." He sighed. "Zachariah, this war, all of it … This is the longest it's taken to resolve."

Dom's gaze softened. "We're doing everything we can to stop him, Greg. You know that."

"But that doesn't matter to the people he's hurt, or to the vampires he's turned against their will. If I can't rehabilitate them, that means more death on my hands." Greg shuddered and took a deep breath. "Those are people who could have been saved had I been able to catch him sooner. And what then?" The muscles in Greg's neck strained, his righteous anger brimming under the surface. "There's always another war, always someone else who wants to raise hell for their ideals. I just want to see it end and stay that way. In the old days, it was easier. Humans were scarcer. A bloodbath could be happening in the village next to them and they wouldn't even know. But now? All of these cities, all of these people?"

Dom shook his head. "It's not the same."

No, it's not. I took on this role to save vampires, not kill them. I don't want to see the people I love hurt. He slumped forward, tired of holding onto this weight, and watched his goddaughter. She ran around the room in joy and delight. Iris warmed his heart, and he thought about the days he wished to have children, the times he'd fallen asleep to those fantasies, to a life with Daniella. But now, he felt as if the chance for that piece of happiness was dangling in front of him, that his fingertips could touch just the end as it threatened to fly away.

"Sometimes it just feels like it's never going to happen," he whispered.

Dom leaned forward in his chair, drawing Greg's gaze. "I can never know the weight of your burdens. You're mindful about keeping them to yourself. One can appreciate that in a leader, but sometimes you need a release. You're not a machine. And I think you're feeling these things because for the first time, you can't stay objective."

Greg's eyes widened at that revelation and the spark it lit with him.

"You know how my life was before I met Merida." Dom's gaze shifted to his daughter as he watched her play, so close to the spitting image of his wife.

Greg nodded. He did. It was the reason he'd picked Dom and Merida to be his seconds-in-command. They knew firsthand what it was like to have the fate of millions resting on their shoulders.

A serene smile graced Dom's face and his eyes were overcome with love for his family. "Somehow, despite everything, I got lucky. I get to call Merida my wife. She has always made me feel alive, and for her I would give the world. She is at the center of my universe, and I'll bet Daniella is at the center of yours."

Greg's gaze shifted away. "She is, but I … Dom if anything ever happens to her." His voice shook.

Dom's eyebrows drew together. "Why are you so sure something will?"

"Because it already did!"

"But that's where you're wrong. She was in danger, but she's not anymore."

"But she could be in the future."

A noise sounded in the corner, drawing both of their gazes as Iris jumped on the floor angrily. "Too loud! Stop mad!" She planted her hands on her hips.

Definitely her mother's daughter. They both chuckled and Iris smiled. Apparently satisfied, she went back to playing.

"Does Merida not have the ability to be in danger in the future? Especially when she refuses to miss a single battle where we're involved? What about me?

What about Iris? Is there not a possibility that someone could hurt her one day? What about my future children? What about yours, Greg?"

Greg's throat tightened at the thought.

"You see, you're stuck feeling afraid of the future because of a horror you experienced in the past. I get it, I understand it. You know I do. But the future isn't set in stone. If you need a reminder of that, think of us," Dom said.

Greg's gaze settled on his clasped hands. *Dom's right, you know he is.* If Greg had been one second later, Merida and Dominick would have died on the docks where he found them with bullets still lodged in their chests. They had believed their lives were going to end that day, but their lives had just begun. The future was always changing for everyone, even him and Daniella.

Dom's voice drew him from his thoughts. "You said you want to build a better future for all of us, and you have. Would it have been lovely if that bastard was dead right now? Of course. But that is not solely your decision. The job you signed up for can seem thankless and difficult, because it is. But do not forget all the people you saved by believing in yourself and the team you've created around you. That was all you, and it will continue to be with your woman by your side."

A beat of pride swelled in Greg's chest. He liked the sound of that. "Thanks, Dom."

Dom shrugged and stood with a smile on his face. "All in a day's work. Now please, cut yourself some slack. I expect you to have the same amount of faith in yourself as we have in you. And if you can't find it, I will be happy to go let my wife know so she can, rightfully, tear you a new asshole."

Iris wagged a finger at her father. "Daddy, bad word! Momma!" she screeched, running towards the door and down the hall.

"And now *I'm* going to get torn a new one too." He smirked. "Don't let my pain be in vain."

Greg laughed as Dominick raced after his daughter. Then he relaxed against the chair, feeling both exhausted and renewed from their conversation. He needed to speak with Daniella, to hear her voice and just … connect with her. He grabbed his phone and called Mya, surprised when Daniella answered instead.

"Greg? Is everything okay?" she asked.

"It is now. I missed you."

He heard her shuffle in the background and then the gentle slide of a chair. "I missed you too." Her voice dropped lower. "It's different without you here."

"I feel the same way." He ruffled his hair. "The meeting took longer than expected. I'd hoped to be on my way back to you by now. I didn't want to leave you, Ella. I'm sorry for not being there when you needed someone."

"No, please, it's okay. I know you didn't want to go, but you had to. And even though you weren't here, you still helped me. What you said before you left … it meant a lot to me."

His heart felt lighter at her words. "It's the truth, you know."

"Greg." She hesitated for a moment. "Come home soon. There's a lot I want to talk to you about, and so much I need to say."

He grabbed his keys in a rush and began packing his bag. "Is everything okay, baby?"

"Yes, I didn't mean to worry you. I just … I'd really like to see you."

He smiled. "You still like the lobster ravioli from Orizzco's, right?"

Daniella laughed, and just hearing the sound warmed his heart. "I do, why?"

"I'll call in an order and pick it up on my way home. It'll take around two hours, but I'll be there as soon as I can."

"You don't have to do that. Plus, it'll be cold by the time it gets here."

He chuckled. "Well lucky for you, I know a thing or two about heating things up."

Her throaty giggle reminded him of how badly he wanted her naked, and he realized too late what he'd insinuated. "Well, I'll be the judge of that when you get here."

"Woman—" he warned.

"Goodbye, Greg." She was still laughing when she hung up.

14

Greg nearly collided with Dom as he opened his door to leave. He took one look at Dom's panicked face and asked, "What's wrong? Did something happen to Iris?"

Dom shook his head. "No, she's fine. Elaine is watching her right now. It's Johanna." Dom motioned for Greg to follow him, and they took the stairs two at a time. "She's the one working with Zachariah."

"What? That doesn't make sense." Johanna, their CHRO, was human, not a being of the otherworld. And if she had been turned, they all would have sensed it.

"Iris' ability gave us a hint," he said in a hushed tone as he opened the door to the administrative level of the building and began checking the offices to make sure they were clear of personnel.

"Merida was checking our HRIS software and scanning employees. Iris saw Johanna's profile and said she didn't like us anymore and that she wasn't 'real'."

Greg unleashed tendrils of his power, using his ability to manipulate matter to check the energy levels of the floor. It was empty. He nodded to Dom, and they approached Johanna's office.

"Merida called Mya. The two of them put their heads together and found a backdoor that had been used to gain access to our databases. The entry point was Johanna's computer."

Greg used his ability again to scan the office. At his confirmation that nothing was out of place, they entered together, and Dominick accessed her computer.

"You know I trust both your judgment and Merida's," Greg said, "but this still doesn't seem right to me. How would she have known how to hack the network and bypass our defenses? We're talking access to the server room, logins, and passwords, and what type of hacking software would we not have been able to catch? All of the tapes were damaged that night. She would have had to know the codes and commands to get into the recording center." He shook his head. "Are we sure no one else was helping her?"

"We're sure now." Merida came in with Luke behind her. "Dom, open her inbox and play the last file from her sent email, please."

He nodded, and they huddled around the screen as Dom double-clicked on the file.

The video started at the front door. A red light flashed as someone swiped their approved keycard to enter the building. It was Johanna, her blonde hair and round glasses reflecting in the overhead lights. Zachariah followed behind her. He smiled directly at the camera, meaning Johanna must have told him where they were.

Zachariah took off in front of her, a blur on the recording, but they all knew what would happen next. The first person murdered was Tony, his body left in the lobby, blood coating the walls. Zachariah moved floor to floor, killing anyone he got his hands on in the blink of an eye. They'd all been newly-turned vampires. They never stood a chance.

Johanna stepped out of the elevator on the fourth floor, missing the carnage. Zachariah dragged Nigel behind him, his face beaten and bloodied. Zachariah's lips moved and Johanna nodded in response before turning away. Zachariah tore into Nigel's throat, ripping apart his skin before he snapped his neck and tossed him to the ground.

Together, they rode the elevator to the eighth floor, the same one Greg and the others were on now. His stomach dropped. He knew who their next victim was. They all did.

Leo, a five-hundred-year-old vampire and one of Greg's battle officers, exited the stairway. He rushed toward Zachariah, knife in hand. Leo was almost on him before he froze mid-assault, paralyzed by an invisible force.

Zachariah placed a small object in Johanna's hand and waved her away. Her steps were robotic, with no trace of recognition or sympathy on her face.

Zachariah took a step towards Leo. His grin spread as he spoke. Then he raised his hand to his throat. They watched on in horror as Leo mimicked the motion, the knife gleaming in the light. Zachariah then pressed two fingers into his skin and smirked as Leo took his own life. He stepped on Leo's crumpled form as if it were nothing but a rug and entered Johanna's office after her. Taking a seat behind her desktop, he slid his hand near the side.

Dom's voice wavered. "I think he's putting in a USB." He nodded to the side of the computer where three ports were located. "Whatever is on that device is how he got into our systems."

"It's almost over," Merida whispered, her voice laced with grief and fury as she squeezed her husband's arm.

Zachariah and Johanna left the office shortly after. They took the elevator to the lobby, but before they left, Zachariah made a call from his cell phone. When a cocky smile appeared on his face, Greg knew exactly who was on the other line.

Daniella.

He'd *visited* her after killing vampires. Greg's vampires. People he cherished and cared for. Greg's body shook with rage. His incisors lengthened and his eyes turned red in fury. The cords of his muscles tightened in preparation for a fight, a battle he waged within himself. This was not the time nor the place, but still it tore through him.

A voice on the computer snapped him back to the present. He focused on the new frame and ground his teeth as he stared right at the face he wanted to crush and burn.

"I hope you enjoyed that little cinematic experience. I have to say, I found it especially compelling." Zachariah tapped his chin. "Ah yes, where are my manners? Greg, how are you doing these days? I assume you're pretty pissed off right now. You know, as a leader, you really should have more security. Or is that the best you could do? That group there was pretty pitiful. It was almost like you left the door wide open for me. Oh, and I must thank you for my fifty-million-dollar gift! Who knew you could be so generous!"

"I'm going to kill him," Luke spat.

"Also, thank you for Johanna. It really is so nice to have friends. It wouldn't have been half as easy without her. Because of her, I now have the addresses of every single member of your little circle. But you know, Greg, killing your vampires gets old after a while. I'd rather convert them, show them the good things in life." Zachariah sat back in his chair. "So, I'll tell you what. You come to these coordinates, offer your head up on a platter, and I'll leave them be. You have twenty-four hours to decide." He sneered. "Don't make me wait."

The video clicked off, and Luke turned and punched the bookcase behind him, sending glass and splinters of wood crashing against the wall.

The action didn't faze Greg, Merida, or Dominick. Greg felt like breaking something himself, but he had to keep it together. They needed to make a plan, and fast.

"Everyone upstairs, now." He turned on his heels and left Johanna's office.

When they reached his office, Greg leaned against his desk. Luke stood near the door, his neck corded, nostrils flared. Greg shook his head, giving him a silent command to behave before addressing Merida and Dominick. "Is there any concern that he got into our offices?"

"No," Merida answered. "Nothing shows that any of the other offices were compromised."

"Good. Since he was in Johanna's office and various areas of the building, I want this building closed tomorrow. Send out a notice to everyone to keep their teams away. Have a sweeper team check for bugs or anything that he could use to gather information."

She nodded.

"As for the addresses—" Greg began.

"The ones in the system are fake. He didn't retrieve anyone's personal information," Dom replied.

"Actually, he could have." Greg drew in a slow breath. "You saw what he did to Nigel. I think he's able to get information by drinking someone's blood. If so, he could have pulled that information from anyone he killed that night."

"And what the fuck was that?" Luke shouted. "What did he do to Leo?"

Greg fought to keep his voice calm, controlled. "I don't know, Luke. I don't know."

"Is there any possibility that those are his new powers?" Dom asked.

Greg shook his head. "No, it's impossible. Zachariah is younger than all of us here. Powers are discovered around every vampire's two hundredth to three hundredth year. He would have just come into his second ability. We already know his first power turns him into a living tank. He couldn't have two additional powers right now."

"Maybe they're not separate powers?"

They all turned their attention to Merida.

"He took information from Nigel through blood. Maybe that's his ability. Maybe part of the information he can take is their power. Or he can copy it. Whatever he used on Leo was some sort of mind control."

"But that wasn't Nigel's ability," Luke spat.

"No, it wasn't," Merida acknowledged. "But if he could control people's minds, including a vampire's, why would he need to threaten Greg? He'd be able to reach any of us at any time. I don't think that ability belongs to him. I think it's something he stole."

"Greg, your ability works similarly, what do you think?" Dom asked.

Greg tapped on the desk in thought. "Whenever I look into a person's memories, it's temporary, and I can't go from one person to another repeatedly without expending a lot of energy. If he's able to control someone's mind, I'd assume the effects would be similar since all of our abilities are tempered in some way." He paused. "I don't think it's a vampire's ability, at least, not one we know. It could belong to a witch, fae, anyone. There are too many variables to guess. But whomever that ability belongs to, they're someone he keeps close. He wouldn't kill them and he wouldn't put them in danger. That ability would be too valuable to him."

"Is it possible," Luke snarled, "that it's Johanna's?"

Dom shook his head. "I don't think so. You saw how she looked throughout the video. I think she was under his control, not the other way around."

"But that doesn't make sense either. She could speak and move around just fine during the meeting on Monday, and she was working today. How would she be able to do that if he was controlling her?" Merida asked.

The door slammed shut as Luke stormed out of Greg's office. Merida and Dominick exchanged looks before turning to face Greg.

"I'll figure out what that was about later." Greg ran his hand through his hair. "For now, let's work on closing everything down. Merida, Dom, I need the two of you to work with Mya on expanding the list of known associates of the vampires that were killed.

I know we have their immediate kin, but I want all family and friends included. Anyone they could have been in contact with within the last six months needs to be moved to another location for their safety. Also, choose a member of your team to investigate what Johanna was working on before she left. Check her employees too."

"And you?" Merida's eyebrow raised. "You're going to the meeting tomorrow, aren't you? Even though you know it's a trap?"

"Of course I am. We've never shied away from a trap before, why start now?" Greg said.

Merida and Dominick stood together. "What time are we having the strategy meeting?"

"Noon, at my house, for now. I'll let you know if that changes."

15

Greg sorted his tasks into a mental list as he drove home. He would call Mya first. She was best at crafting the most effective routes, entry, and exit points, and would be key in ensuring their team would arrive safely at Zachariah's coordinates.

It was also an excuse to speak with Daniella. His mind was going a mile a minute, and he needed to hear her voice, to feel something of her wash over him. He dialed Mya's phone number and, just as before, Daniella answered instead. Her voice filled his ears and everything else stilled.

Greg explained they'd found out Johanna was working with Zachariah, and he apologized for yet another delay. She absorbed the information and told him to take care on his way home, that she would be there, waiting for him.

Waiting for him. Against the odds, he smiled.

He relayed the same information to Mya. She had already received the coordinates from Merida and had begun analyzing.

After their call, Greg contacted each of his battle officers and provided them with the details of their emergency strategy meeting. He did all of this while monitoring the road to ensure he wasn't being followed. That was part of the reason why he'd chosen a property so far away from the office. The long drive meant many side streets and alternate routes home if needed. It also provided him with plenty of ways to lose someone if they were tailing him, including using his ability to flip their car and kill them without ever leaving his seat. He hadn't been followed in quite some time, but after the stunt Zachariah had pulled at his office, Greg couldn't take any chances.

Finally, he called Luke. It had been over an hour since he'd walked out of Greg's office, and he hoped his cousin had calmed down by now.

"Hey," Luke said.

Greg breathed a sigh of relief when he answered. "Hey. Is now a good time?"

"Yeah." There was a small rustling on the other end of the line before Luke continued, his voice heavy. "I'm sorry for storming off on you. That was inexcusable."

Greg ran his fingers through his hair. "Luke, I love you like a brother, but I cannot help you if you do not tell me what is going on. I understand your anger, but that was something else."

He sighed. “I know. But I can’t, not yet. I’m confused. None of it makes any sense, and I just … I don’t know what’s going on Greg. I just don’t know.”

“Is it Johanna?”

Luke drew in a harsh breath.

“I know you thought she would be a good fit for the team,” Greg said, remembering his feedback after her interview.

“That’s not … it.”

When Luke chose not to explain further, Greg tapped the steering wheel and let out a deep sigh. “Whatever it is, I won’t push you. When you’re ready, come to me. We’ll sit down and work this out together, okay? But whatever is causing you to feel however you do, it’s not your fault. What is that ridiculousness you’re always preaching to me? ‘I can only control what I do or don’t do, nothing else’.”

Luke laughed. “The world must have gone to shit if you’re quoting my advice back to me.”

Greg shrugged, chuckling. “Nah. I just wanted you to realize I do actually listen to you, so you would quit your whining one of these days.”

“Asshole.”

“I learned from the best.” Greg grinned. “We’re having the meeting tomorrow at noon. I’ll see you then.”

“Okay. And Greg? Thanks for always being there for me.”

“Of course. We’re family.”

The sound of laughter greeted Greg as he entered his home. It brought a smile to his face, which widened when he noticed the lights were on, welcoming him inside. Daniella really had waited for him, and that knowledge squeezed his heart, sending warmth through his chest.

When he entered the kitchen, Daniella's eyes met his and lit up. A smile formed across her lips and her shoulders visibly relaxed. "Welcome home."

Greg set the bags of food on the counter. With them out of the way, he could finally see all of her. He stopped dead in his tracks. Her t-shirt and shorts combination left her skin exposed, and he could see the new wounds that marred her skin: a cut on one arm, another across her chest, and her knuckles were purple, a bruise already forming.

What the fuck? Greg didn't hear Mya's sarcastic remarks, didn't even see her as his vision homed in on Daniella.

He pulled her to him and then lifted her over his shoulder. Daniella squealed and yelled his name, but it didn't deter him. He carried her out of the room and sprinted down the hall. When he reached the bathroom, he slammed the door shut and pinned her against it.

Daniella gasped and placed her hands on his chest, but he responded with a snarl, a warning. His breathing was rapid, harsh. Greg lifted one of her legs, holding the base of her foot as his eyes raked over her skin. His hand slid up her ankle, then her calf, following the path to her thigh before pausing at another wound.

He ground his teeth but continued until he reached her hip. He did the same thing to her other leg and found a bruise on her foot and another on her hip.

When he spoke, his tone was low, threatening. "Where did these come from?"

Daniella shifted her gaze from his. The scent of her arousal washed over him as she trembled and clutched at his shoulders. Greg's nostrils flared as he continued his inspection under her shirt. His heartbeat was so loud that he almost missed her answer.

"I was training with Mya."

Greg froze. "You were what? Daniella, you are a human. We are vampires. There is no need for you to do any sort of training."

She pushed against his chest, but he refused to allow any distance between them and instead pressed his body harder against hers. The way she moaned his name made him growl.

"Greg," she tried again. "I have to learn how to protect myself."

"God damnit, Daniella! No, you don't. You are mine!" He growled, pinning her hands above her head. "You are mine to protect, mine to take care of, my priority. You are my mate. If you wanted to learn how to protect yourself so badly, you should have come to me!"

Daniella shivered, but even her haze of desire couldn't hide the defiance in her eyes. "If I would have gone to you, you would do the same thing you're doing *right* now. The moment I got hurt, you'd call the whole thing off. I needed to learn something!" Her voice softened. "You shouldn't have to take care of me. I can't be your priority. Your circle is your priority, and I want to help you with that, not hinder you."

Her words hit him like a blow, taking all of his anger and rage and leaving him scared and broken. He curved until his forehead rested against hers. "You are my priority."

"Greg—"

"You're my priority because the circle can survive on its own, but I can't survive without you."

She gasped, her body still against his.

"Ella, is it so wrong for me to want to be everything you need? Everything you want? To give you everything you could ever desire?" He cupped her face. "Seeing you hurt destroys me."

"No, it's not wrong." She wrapped her arms around his neck, and her smile could have rivaled the sun. "But you've forgotten one thing. You already are all of those things for me, *my* everything."

Greg's lips clashed against hers. He pulled her to him, pushed against her. They twisted, yanked, fell against one another like a rising tide, but it wasn't enough. He'd gotten a taste of her, the way she felt when she'd allowed him to wander, and now he wanted more.

He kissed down the contours of her neck. Daniella held him close as he sucked and nibbled on her. When he bit her neck, stopping himself from puncturing her skin, she moaned.

"Soon," he whispered against her flesh, a promise to the both of them.

Daniella fisted his shirt, clutching him to her. "Greg, please."

"Don't worry, love. I'm not going to stop, not yet." He licked down to her breast and traced the already fading scar with his tongue.

She sucked in a breath, tangling her hand in his hair. "But Mya—"

He pulled his head back for a moment, and her whine of protest made him smile. Greg lowered the straps of her top and bra until her beautiful breasts were free for him to savor.

"When I'm inside of you," he began, trailing kisses around the mound as his hand slid over her stomach, "I will make you scream my name. But for now"—his fingers slid under her shorts and pressed between her lips, tracing her core through her underwear, making her gasp—"I need you to stay quiet for me. I don't want anyone to interrupt us, not until I make you come. Can you be quiet, Ella?"

She bit her lip, nodding in response as he pushed her underwear to the side and circled her clit. He sucked her nipple into his mouth and watched as her head fell back against the door. Over and over, he thumbed the engorged nub, adding pressure slowly while he teased her breast, switching from one delicious mound to the other.

Greg slid his finger down lower and then pushed inside of her. She covered her mouth, moaning against her palm. He thrust inside, rubbing her sensitive bud, keeping his movements in sync. When she rocked her hips, he slid another digit into her wet heat. Daniella gasped, sinking down, taking him deeper.

He let her breast go and claimed her mouth. Using the new angle, Greg curled his fingers, increasing his speed as he devoured each and every single one of her cries.

She clung to him, wrapping her legs around his waist, her arms squeezing his back. Greg rolled and pinched her nipple, and she grew wilder at the mixture of pain and pleasure. She was so fucking wet that it took everything in him not to ram inside of her. But he needed this, needed her, needed to give her pleasure. It was the only thing that would appease the animal inside of him.

She shivered as her movements became chaotic and disjointed. "Yes, yes, *yes!*" Daniella cried into his neck, sucking on his skin as he groaned. Then she trembled. Her head snapped back and she froze, suspended in bliss. He kissed her, swallowing her cries as she came, her liquid drenching his fingers as her pussy spasmed around him. Still he moved his fingers slowly, in and out, until her body relaxed, and then he withdrew them from her.

With a smile, he sucked them into his mouth and moaned at her taste. "I always knew you would be delicious."

They shuffled back into the kitchen together. Greg's hair was out of place, still a mess from Daniella's fingers, and she'd ripped several of the buttons off his shirt, but he didn't care. They were his own personal gifts, brands from the woman he loved.

Mya's gaze went from his face to Daniella's and back before she cackled. "You guys could have at least waited until I left to have sex, jeez."

"Come on, sis, you know I don't do anything half-ass."

Mya was still chuckling as she left the kitchen, and Greg used the opportunity to spread his fingers over Daniella's stomach and whisper in her ear, "You wouldn't be able to walk if we did."

A blush crept over her skin and she shivered. She smacked at his hand. "Arrogance doesn't become you."

Greg smirked as they sat at the table. "It isn't arrogance if it's the truth." He grasped her chin in his hand. "If you like, I'd be more than happy to prove it to you. Right here, right now."

He kissed down her neck while his hand slid up her thigh. "Would you let me bend you over this table and fuck you, Ella?"

Her pulse raced under his lips, but when he pulled back, he saw her devilish grin. She grasped his wrist, stopping his advance. "Two can play that game, Gregori. After all"—her fingers fell to his lap—"with how hard you are, it would be so easy to make a mess of you."

He squeezed her wrist before she was able to touch him. "I'll remember that for later, vixen."

Mya returned with two large maps. "If you two are done doing whatever you're doing over there, I pulled up those coordinates you gave me." She unrolled the maps and arranged them on the table before tapping on an area west of NYC. "I believe it's an unmarked cavern. I don't have a lot to base that hunch off of, but there's a cave system less than two miles away."

"So we have no way to determine how many entrances or exits there are, which means they can attack from anywhere." Greg paused, making a mental note of the roads in and out of that location and how easy it would be for a vampire to travel on foot. "I think Zachariah would attack from inside the cavern where he'd have more control. If he swarms from the outside, we'd have an easier chance to either overwhelm him or flee than if we're stuck in a tight space or driven further into a location we know nothing about."

Mya nodded. "What's the plan?"

"The same as always. We go in."

She raised an eyebrow. "Even though we're sure it's a trap?"

The air around Daniella tingled, calling Greg's focus. Small, almost invisible lines curved and rubbed against themselves, creating a type of pulse in the air that shimmered. His gaze shifted back to Mya, but she seemed to be entirely immune to the experience. Perhaps he could only feel it due to his abilities, or his proximity to Daniella. It wasn't a negative feeling, the opposite, in fact. It felt comforting, like a mother's hand on her child guiding them down an unknown path.

Perhaps it was the voices she had mentioned. Could they be revealing something to her about the location? About him? Unsure of what to do, he carefully wrapped his arm around her to remind her he was there if she needed him. But she didn't move, didn't even blink, her blank stare focused on the map.

With a sigh, he finally responded to Mya. "Especially since we're sure it's a trap. We have a reason to make sure we can keep him and his vampires in that space as well. If they get out, we'll lose them. The best strategy we have at this point is offense. He wants a battle, so we'll bring it to him. That's our chance of victory."

Daniella blinked, coming out of her trance, and Greg shifted as she leaned against him. "Are you okay?" he asked.

Her eyes had grown red and her heartbeat thundered so loud he thought she was going to have another anxiety attack. She grabbed hold of him and pulled him towards her until she could meet his lips. Her kiss was desperate, as if she were begging the gods to freeze time right at this moment.

When he pulled away from her, breathless, he saw fresh tears in her eyes. "Ella? What's wrong?"

"I'm okay. I'll tell you tomorrow." Her gaze slid to Mya. "Can we talk about all of this tomorrow? Please?"

Mya, just as confused as he was, tilted her head to the side but nodded. "Of course."

Greg cradled Daniella, and she clung to him, grasping his back in her tiny hands.

Mya searched Greg's gaze for answers, but all he could do was shrug and shake his head. She folded the maps to clear off the table. "Why don't we eat and try to enjoy the night then?"

Daniella's shoulders slumped in relief. "Thank you."

They ate and fell into an easy conversation around the table with light teasing and small laughs, but eventually the night came to an end.

They stood and Greg pulled his cell phone out of his pocket. "Do you mind if I make a couple of calls?"

Daniella smiled. "No, I'll see Mya out. I have a few things to discuss with her anyway."

Greg looked between the two of them. The smirk on Mya's lips did not bode well for him.

"There's no need for you to worry, big bro. At least, not yet." Mya's smile spread and Daniella laughed.

"I wasn't until you said that, little sister." He gave her a hug. "Be careful on your way home. Text me when you get there, and if you can, please don't corrupt my mate's mind before you leave."

"I can't make any promises."

Greg chuckled and dropped a kiss on Daniella's head. "I'll be in the study when you're done."

16

Greg was on his last call when Daniella entered the room, dressed in a floor-length silk robe. Everything faded away as he took her in, catching the mischievous look in her eyes and the teasing smile that played on her lips.

She had tied the robe around her waist loose enough for it to fall open and give him a generous view of her skin. He followed it with his eyes, devouring the path between her breasts, over her stomach, and down to her navel, disappointed when the sash obstructed his further progression.

With each step, the robe opened, revealing her long legs. The soft fragrance of her shower gel as it mixed in with her natural scent wrapped around him, tantalizing his senses. Saliva pooled in his mouth and he barely caught himself before he drooled.

Her smile grew, and his cock hardened. His vixen knew exactly what she was doing, seducing him.

There was a murmur on the other end of the phone with an uptake at the end. A question. "What?" he asked Michael.

"I asked how many people you want to watch the Tompson building."

"Five." Greg swallowed hard as she sat on the couch. The robe draped open around her as she crossed her legs and folded her hands over her knee. He wanted to be in between those legs, to feel them wrapped around his waist, or better yet, his head as he teased her clit.

Is she naked under that robe? Please, gods, let her be naked.

She had his sole focus, and he knew he had to give up when he missed something else Michael said. "I think we're having some interference. I'll conference you in at noon, alright?"

"Okay, Greg. Talk to you then."

"Bye." He hung up and rose from his chair, dropping the phone onto his desk.

Two can play this game. Greg's hands slid to the top of his shirt, releasing the first button from its closure, then the next, and the next, smirking as Daniella watched him. Her eyes heated, darkening to near black, and when she licked her lips, he almost groaned.

"Were you really getting interference?" she whispered, breathless.

"Yes, due to the gorgeous woman who walked into my office." He unbuckled his belt and ripped it free from the loops, throwing it on the ground as he prowled toward her.

She bit her lip, trying to suppress her whimper. But he caught its melody in the air as he grasped her chin, forcing her to meet his eyes.

"I am going to worship you like the goddess you are."

Greg pulled her onto his lap. Her gasp turned into a moan as he kissed her neck, tracing her skin with his tongue. Her arms wrapped around him while he pulled at the ends of the robe, desperate to feel her, touch her anywhere, to sate his curiosity.

His hands slid up her calves, caressing her skin. She was so soft, so smooth, like butter, and he was starving, famished for a taste of her. Then he reached her thighs, pulling the material caught from between their rolling hips, and when her heat brushed against his pants, he nearly lost his mind. Daniella was naked, wet, and wanting, all for him.

Her hand slid down his body, following the panes of his chest, over his abs, reaching the waistband of his pants where his cock strained to break free. That was his last barrier, after that …

"Daniella, I won't be able to stop."

"Who said I want you to?" Her fingertips brushed over the closure and he hissed as she lowered the zipper.

"You'll be immortal." He growled as she licked her beautiful, heart-shaped lips, drawing his gaze. Greg had to say this now, while he still could. "You'll be stronger, faster, you won't age—"

She palmed him through his boxers and he cursed, a moan escaping his lips.

"On my first night here, you asked me if I could accept you, all of you, and my answer has never changed. Not once. It's always been yes to everything, including becoming immortal if it means I get to be with you."

Her hands left his body and he mourned the loss until they moved to her sash. Greg's breath caught as she pulled it free.

"I've always been yours, Gregori." Daniella rolled her shoulders and the robe dropped, pooling around them and leaving her glorious body on full display. "So take me."

He crushed his lips against hers and pushed her back onto the couch. He wallowed in the softness of her skin, in the warmth of her body. Greg brushed her hair back, his fingers buried in it as he grasped her head and kept her lips lined against his while he consumed her. His tongue entered the warmth of her mouth and he moaned as she met each stroke.

Her hands were restless over his body, moving, groping, squeezing at his skin. Daniella branded him with each touch, and he reacted the same. He nestled between her legs, forcing them wider, and she cradled him there. His erection, already pulsing and heavy, fit against her as he ground his hips. He drank in every moan, felt dizzy as her wetness seeped through his boxers.

Fuck. He was drowning, and he hadn't even touched her yet.

Greg slid his hands down her body and she curved into his touch. He loved her moans, loved how responsive she was. When he reached her clit and circled the nub, she moaned and spread her legs wider to accept him. She *accepted* him, and it drove him crazy.

His teeth scraped over her nipple before he closed his lips around it, sucking it into his mouth, toying with it. Daniella writhed beneath him. He slid one finger and then another into her wet heat, moaning at how she drenched his hand.

She cursed and moaned as his fingers rocked inside of her. Daniella tilted her hips to draw his fingers in further as she ground against his palm, begging for release, and when he curled his fingers and thumbed her clit, she did.

Her cries urged him. He needed to see her orgasm again, to leave her a sweaty, disjointed mess for him to touch, taste, tease. *All for him.*

By the time his mouth made it down to her hips, her breathing was erratic. He paused at the junction of her thighs and watched with heated fascination as his fingers slid in and out of her, coated in her juices. The sight was beautiful, and he couldn't stop himself from sliding them into his mouth and sucking them clean.

"Greg," she panted, watching him.

He traced the inside of her thighs with his tongue and she squirmed from his touch. As he grew closer to her core, her breaths became shallower, rushed, and he smiled in pure satisfaction. Then he blew on her pussy before taking the lips into his mouth. She clung onto the arm of the couch, arching her back as he sucked once, twice, before spreading her lips with his tongue and sliding inside. He moaned at her taste, even more so when her climax hit her again.

But he didn't stop, couldn't. Not until she was grasping at his hair, both pushing and tugging the strands as she went wild underneath him. Not until her thighs squeezed tightly around his head, until her pelvis moved in perfect harmony with the strokes of his tongue.

When he touched her engorged clit, applying the familiar pressure she loved before easing away, she hissed and he chuckled. He enjoyed teasing her, especially when he knew she was so close. Leaving her sweet pussy, he kissed her clit, drew it into his mouth and sucked, sliding two fingers inside of her again.

Daniella's hips lifted off the couch when she came hard, tensing every part of her body as her release flew through her. She cried out, moaning his name.

I want to hear her scream it.

The single thought pushed the rest of his blood to his cock. Greg tore at his clothes, desperate to free himself and finally penetrate her. Daniella gasped at the sight of him. Her eyes roamed over his form, pausing at his dick.

When he settled himself in between her legs, she sat up and stopped him. "I want to taste you." She coated her fingers in his pre-cum and spread it over his dick, before gripping him in both hands.

His head fell back as pleasure soared through his body, and when she took him inside of her perfect little mouth, he swore he saw stars. "Fuck, Ella."

She looked up at him, her eyes dark and devious as she sucked more of him in until he hit the back of her throat. His eyes closed, hands fisting the couch as she relaxed her throat to take him as deep as she could. Greg used every shred of his control to resist fisting her hair and thrusting inside of her throat, but when she clutched at his ass and pushed, he gave her what they both wanted.

She moaned, the vibration wrapping around his cock, and he shuddered as he thrust again. Daniella cupped his balls as she let him use her mouth, moaning with him, deriving pleasure from his own.

She made him crazy. He couldn't take it anymore. Daniella whined as he pulled away from her. Greg dragged her hips to his, and she gasped as he forced her onto her back. With one deep thrust, he was finally, *finally* inside of her.

"Is this what you wanted?" he growled.

"Yes! Yes!"

Greg angled her hips, stuffing a pillow underneath her as he rammed home again. Her hands kneaded his back, nails raking over his skin, and he squeezed her hips, pounding faster. He pushed into her, driving them higher as she clung to him. "Mine!"

He sucked her neck, his fangs dancing along her skin. He'd hid them for as long as he could, but now he was too far gone. The need to slip them into her skin and taste her, *claim* her, make her his, was irresistible.

When she tilted her neck to the side, gripping his hair, he surrendered. He bit her, moaning as her blood flowed into his mouth and he sucked her life's essence into him, completing their bond.

Daniella cried out, chanting his name as he picked up pace. The world had disappeared, and it was only them, only this feeling. Nothing existed outside of their bodies. The way her walls spasmed around his cock, taking him deeper, the way her fingers gripped and slid over his skin until she scratched his back, how she held him, how the scent of their sex permeated the air, was everything. Nothing could ever match this feeling, nothing could ever make him feel so damn whole, so damn *good.*

He fucked her until he was senseless, and then he felt it for the first time. The shiver that coursed through her body, the way her breath caught in her throat as she prepared for one last scream, and it was his name on her lips as her pussy spasmed around his cock. His eyes rolled back as she dragged him over the edge.

Greg pulled his teeth out of her neck a moment before he shouted, his orgasm rolling through him like a freight train as he filled her to the brim.

17

When morning came and she'd finally left Greg's warm embrace, Daniella felt relaxed. One could even say sated, as long as she managed not to stay too close to him, think about him too often, or what they had spent most of the night and early morning doing.

Making love with Greg was everything she could have asked for and then some. According to him, it had also made her immortal. She was still human, but taking Greg as her mate gave her certain vampiric abilities, such as strength, speed, and immunity.

Daniella didn't feel any different, although Mya's movements seemed slower to her, like if she focused just enough, she could catch them out of the corner of her eye. Sometimes it even seemed like she hit harder, but true to Mya's word, even if she did, Mya would still have the upper hand. She was trained and honed for battle in a way Daniella was not, but she would be. She *would* be.

"Remember to widen your stance. If you don't, you'll leave your left side open," Mya said, pulling her from her thoughts.

Daniella grunted and spread her legs further apart.

Mya spun to kick her again. Daniella knew she wouldn't be able to miss the attack, so she crossed her arms and blocked it.

"Good." Mya nodded. "You're faster. Mating with my brother agrees with you."

Daniella blushed, but stayed focused. She threw out a jab, and then another.

Mya evaded both and returned the attack.

Daniella ducked, escaping the first two punches, but Mya's elbow hit home. Her connection with the water spirit may have kept her from feeling pain, but the hit would definitely leave a bruise tomorrow.

Daniella's magic was where her strength lay. With it, she could unleash devastating long-range attacks. But she had to stay balanced and could only do so if she learned how to defend herself in close combat. If someone could incapacitate her, she would be nothing but a liability.

They practiced for another hour before switching techniques.

"Do you want to work on the boiling my blood thing again? I'm quite amused by it."

Daniella side-eyed her. "You're a masochist."

"Don't judge." Mya winked and they shared a laugh. "Plus, if I remember correctly, you had fun setting me on fire yesterday."

Daniella scrunched her nose. "Please, you know how much I hated that. No one likes the smell of burnt flesh."

Mya shrugged. "You'll have to get used to it though. Setting a vampire on fire may save your life in the future, and at least it's something if you can't figure out how to get the blood boiling to work, especially on such short notice."

Daniella sighed. "You're right."

They'd spent a large part of yesterday planning and testing her powers. While her abilities were strong, much like a vampire's, she was not all powerful. Daniella could only affect an area she knew or could see. Because of that, a cavern with unknown, winding tunnels would hinder her, and she could not use any type of field magic or else she may injure their allies during the fight. Her only option was individualized magic that focused on the vampire's body.

"Are you sure that your healing ability will counter my magic?" she asked.

Mya laced her fingers, pushing at her wrists for a stretch. "I'll be fine, just try it already. But remember, focus on the brain. Anywhere else won't kill us."

Daniella nodded and closed her eyes. She connected to her surroundings and pushed deeper, past the cool breeze that dried her sweat, the warmth of the sun, and the wetness that hung in the air. Past the skin, outside of the natural world. There she pondered. What was she missing? Why couldn't she affect Mya's blood and heat it?

Perhaps it was her doubt and fear. Fear of hurting her friend, fear of this not working, the small voice that told her this was too sudden and much too new for her to be an expert at. While her fears may be justified, they frankly didn't matter. If she couldn't figure out how to defend herself and kill vampires, Mya would never help her make it to tonight's battle, and she had to, or else … *No!* She could not think about that now.

With renewed determination, she focused on her intent. Another deep breath released any lingering emotions, leaving her open to receiving and listening to the spirits. Then an idea popped into her head, single and certain. *Dehydration!* If she removed water from Mya's body, it would overheat.

Daniella called to the spirit that ebbed and flowed, equally calm and yet able to rupture and crash at any moment. She gasped at the surge of power, at how it wound around her and merged with her desire so seamlessly that it felt like a part of her consciousness. She was so engrossed in this feeling that she missed Mya's groan, the way she couldn't lift her tongue to speak, and how she swayed in the yard, until she heard a loud *thump.*

Daniella opened her eyes to see Mya on the ground. She rushed to her and cradled Mya's head to her chest. "Mya? Mya! Are you okay?"

Mya groaned in response.

Daniella released the breath she'd been holding. "Fuck, I'm so sorry."

Mya waived her hand dismissively and began to sit up on her own. She let Daniella help her to her feet, and they moved to a nearby bench. Daniella offered Mya her bottled water, but she shook her head, bracing her hands on her knees.

After several deep breaths, Mya slumped back against the seat with a sigh, eyes closed. "Well, it's good to know that works."

"Are you sure you're alright? Do you need me to get you anything?"

"No, I'm okay. I've almost finished healing." She opened her eyes to peer at Daniella. "Stop worrying before you end up with a permanent crease in the middle of your forehead. I'm fine. Now, do you think you can do that on a massive scale?"

She scowled. "Yes, Madam Dickness."

Mya's roar of laughter made Daniella smile, easing a bit of her guilt. She sat back against the seat and stared at the sky. Hurting Mya like that, so easily, shocked her. The spirits didn't operate on the same scale as humans, where everything was black and white, just or unjust. Death didn't harm them, nor did life bring them joy. They had no qualms about peace or destruction, and the more she connected to them, the easier it was to succumb to their force and forget the world existed. Daniella had to be clear about her boundaries when working with them, or else she may hurt someone she loved in the future.

Her gaze shifted back to Mya, who was staring off into the distance, toying with something on a small chain around her neck. The object shone in the light and Daniella realized it was a ring, a simple golden band that seemed too big for Mya's long fingers.

Noticing she was being watched, Mya stopped and laid the ring flat against her chest. "Greg is going to fight you with everything he has when you tell him you want to join us at the battle tonight. I want you to understand why."

Daniella cocked her head to the side but nodded. "Okay."

Mya struggled for a while to find the words, and when she finally did, she seemed broken. "I wasn't … always this way. Cruel and brash, I mean. I've always been stubborn, hard-headed, a pain in the ass." She gave a sad smile. "But this, who I am today, was born out of pain and loss."

"I never agreed with Greg keeping you in the dark about us, because you should value the time you have with your mate. You never know when you might lose them." Mya picked up the ring again, grasping it in her hand. "This belonged to him, my mate, but he's gone now. This is one of the only things I have left of him."

Daniella's eyes widened. She reached out to hold Mya's hand as a tear slid down her friend's cheek. "Mya, I—"

"It's okay. I don't talk about him often, but it's nice to remember." Mya sniffled. "My parents were the epitome of love, and they did everything they could to teach us those values, to keep us connected. But when I was a child, they contracted the plague, and I lost both of them."

Daniella nodded. "Greg told me about the plague. That you got it as well, and how Erik turned him into a vampire, and then Greg turned you and Luke."

Mya's face warmed and for a moment her eyes brightened. "When I met Erik, he looked like an angel. I was dying. I knew it. I could feel the energy slipping from my body. When Erik taught Greg how to turn me into a vampire, he said Greg should be the one to do it because I had the greatest connection with him. But that wasn't true." She squeezed the ring again. "The person I had the greatest connection with was Erik. I just didn't know it at the time."

Daniella shook her head. "I don't understand."

"Erik was my mate, Dani."

She gasped and drew back. "But how? Greg told me he lost his mate. How could you be his mate?"

"We stayed with Erik for hundreds of years. Vampires stop growing in their twenties, and when he met me, I was only five years old. He helped me grow, not only as a vampire, but as a child. I treated him like a father figure at first." She laughed. "I'd cling to him constantly, always begging for him to play with me or carry me around town. When I was scared, I'd run to him. He was my safe place." The tears flowed freely now, but she wiped them away and took a deep, shuddering breath. "That changed when I became older. Erik taught us how to fight, how to survive. He talked to us about our powers and abilities. But even though our bodies had matured as humans, we still had a lot to learn as vampires. I saw him differently then, but I never acted on it." She breathed. "He saved my life. He helped raise me. I just … I didn't think it was appropriate, and yet I couldn't let it go."

Daniella wished she could take a piece of Mya's pain, but she couldn't. Its claws were too deep into her for Daniella to begin to help her heal, but still she tried as she rubbed her back, sending her all the comfort and light that she could through her touch while she listened to her story.

"We went through many wars together. That's why we came to America. We believed that it would be easier here, and over time Erik and I grew closer. But there were other beings here, ones that did not appreciate all the turmoil humans, and some vampires, had brought. Two of them could shape-shift, mimic another person's body and their mannerisms perfectly, and that's what they did. They tricked him into thinking I'd rejected him completely, and it broke his heart."

Mya's lip trembled and she bit it to keep from sobbing. "I didn't even know! He never told me about mates. I had never even heard the term before. I just … I just knew I felt something different with him than anyone else did. I wanted something more with him. He left me a journal filled with entries about me. About how I'd grown, how hard it was to stay away from me, how happy he had been that we were advancing toward a relationship, all the hopes and dreams he had for a future with me. He left me this"—she kissed the ring softly—"and then he left me." Her eyes hardened. "That's what happens when your mate rejects you as an immortal being. The emptiness is too much to bear, and it's easier to die."

Tears had already gathered in Daniella's eyes, but it wasn't until Mya shut down that they began their descent down her cheeks. Mya brushed away her lingering tears, straightened her back, and held her head high. Not a trace of the vulnerable woman who had been crying and talking about the love of her life was left. She had been replaced with a warrior, someone who could kill without consequence. It shook Daniella down to her core.

"I killed them. I killed every person who helped take him away from me, who burnt down his house and left me with nothing. Their lives for his, and I would do it again in a heartbeat," she spat. "Had it not been for Greg and Luke holding me back and nursing me through the pain, I would have followed Erik in death. Our bond ran that deep, and we had never even consummated it, unlike you and my brother."

Daniella's heart jumped, the ache reverberating through her body leaving her speechless as her eyes widened.

"You understand what I'm saying, don't you? I agreed I would bring you to tonight's battle, even against my brother's wishes, because your spirits told you he would die if you were not there to prevent it. But there will be no room for sympathy there.

Nothing will exist except for action and instinct. The only mentality you should have is kill or be killed. If you cannot watch the life slip from someone's eyes to save your own, or my brother's, then it's better that you let him die in peace." Mya's voice wavered, but nevertheless she sat tall. "Because if he survives you, he will do exactly as I did. He will destroy everything, and he will choose to follow you to the grave. Nothing I, or anyone else, could do will convince him otherwise." She squeezed Daniella's shoulder. "Make sure your heart is in the right place before you leave with us tonight."

Daniella broke apart. Tears muddied her face as she sobbed at the cruel honesty of Mya's words. She was right. Hadn't Greg confessed the same thing yesterday? That he couldn't survive without her? And after last night…

She shook her head, wanting to drown out the thought, but it wouldn't leave her. Greg wouldn't survive her death. He wouldn't even try to, and she couldn't accept that. She knew how she felt about Greg. She loved him with everything in her. Wasn't that the reason she was going through with all of this? If Mya was asking her if she could kill someone to protect Greg, the answer would always be yes.

But didn't that make her a monster?

What was the point of no return?

When did justice and protection turn you into a murderer?

Zachariah was a murderer. He took people's lives for fun. He didn't care about anything other than himself.

And her? What did she care about?

The answer was simple. Greg. Daniella cared about the man she loved. She cared about Luke and Mya. She even cared about the other vampires, people that she didn't know. There was no reason for them to be involved in this madness.

Was that it, then? Was that the line between good and evil?

The phrase 'for the greater good' came to the forefront of her mind. Daniella had always hated that phrase, yet never understood why until this very moment. The choice of what was the greater good was always subjective and thus selfish. But that changed nothing for her.

She may be partial. She may be selfish. But to her, the greater good was Greg and his family. It was what he was doing, what all of them did. No matter the circumstances, on any day, at any part of her life, she would always choose him over another. And if that made her evil, so be it. If that meant watching somebody die in front of her, no matter how difficult that may be, no matter how hard it may be for her to wrap her mind around, he was worth it. They were worth it.

18

Greg's voice rang strong and clear as Daniella entered the house. Luke said something, and he laughed, a deep masculine rumble that danced over her skin. The thought of never hearing his voice again—

Her power ripped through her with such strength that she barely stopped herself from setting his home aflame. Shaken, she wrapped her arms around herself. She couldn't fall apart here, not with so much on the line.

Daniella raced upstairs and peeled off her clothes. She made it into the shower before she curled into a ball and smothered a scream with her hand. Her thoughts had turned into a chaotic web of despair. What if she couldn't convince him? What if she couldn't stop whatever was coming? What if she lost him? What if, what if, what if?

Stop! Stop, this isn't you. You always push through, you always do, and this isn't any different.

She repeated her mother's mantra in her head, let it fill her with peace as she grounded her energy. *I am one with the earth. I am one with the Mother. She flows through me. She offers me her guidance, and I can make it through anything.*

Her breathing calmed and her pulse slowed until she could think straight. She had suffered a great deal of hardship and loss in her life, and that unresolved pain had created a chasm of fear. Fear that she wasn't strong enough to protect someone she loved, fear that she'd lose someone else. But if she was willing to risk her life for Greg's, and even kill someone if necessary, the least she could do was believe in herself and her magic. The spirits said she would bring him home, and she *would.*

As she washed, Daniella imagined each negative thought leaving her body, swirling into the water and spiraling down the drain. When she finished, she wrapped herself in a towel and cleared the mirror of condensation. Brown eyes stared back at her, red where the whites should be and somewhat shifty, but otherwise clear and determined.

Tingles raced down her skin when Greg entered the bathroom, and her body hummed a soft melody of completion when his arms came around her. She couldn't resist melting into his embrace as he pressed himself against her.

“Hi,” he whispered in her ear, eliciting a wave of goosebumps over her body. His eyes were dark and hungry in the mirror as he nestled the bulge of his dick between her ass cheeks. “I missed you.”

Liquid heat pooled at her core and she sighed. “I missed you too.”

She slid her nails down his arm and he hissed. His fingers brushed over her neck, tracing the path down to her shoulder and over the wound Mya had inflicted during their training. “I hate seeing these on you,” he said gruffly, softly licking the wound, healing it.

Daniella whimpered. Her head fell back as he trailed kisses over her shoulder and back up her neck. Greg’s hands roamed over her body. He squeezed her breast, and even through the towel she could feel the heat of his palm. She moaned and clutched at his hand. She could get lost in him, *lost*—

“Wait!”

He let go of her breast and loosened his grip as she turned to face him.

Daniella rubbed her hands over his chest. “We need to talk.”

“What’s wrong, baby?” Concern filled his eyes as he smoothed her hair, brushing the loose strands behind her ear before his hands fell to her hips.

“I’m going with you tonight.”

“No,” he said flatly, “you’re not.”

“Greg, please listen to me.”

“No, Daniella.” His hands tightened on her waist. “As much as I hate to admit it, you were right about learning how to defend yourself. But I will not let you follow me or anyone else into battle. I will not let you willingly put yourself in a position where you could get hurt. I love you too much for that."

Her heart stopped. He'd told her in so many other ways, but hearing those three little words took all of her fight and replaced it with a gentle understanding. Daniella slid her hand up to his cheek. "My love—"

Greg's eyes widened and he shook his head as if tormented. "No, please … please don't call me that. It's already too hard to say no to you. Please don't tempt me this way."

She smiled and cupped his cheek. "My love, I need you to listen to me, please."

He treated the soft caress as if it was his salvation. His eyes drifted closed and he nuzzled her palm, tickling her skin with his stubble.

"I love you," she whispered.

His eyes snapped open.

"We're in the same boat. We feel the same way about one another, and I don't want to lose you. But if I don't go with you tonight, I will, and I'm not willing to let that happen."

Greg trembled as he spoke, his tone low, dark. "And how do you know this? Why are you so sure?"

"Because the spirits told me last night when Mya opened the map. They warned me you would not come back to me if I did not go with you."

His jaw clenched, but she continued on before he could protest. "I did not agree to spend my life with you, only to lose you so quickly. I understand you want to protect me. I also understand why you refuse to budge, but you need to understand that I will not either. Compromise with me." She stroked his cheek.

"Ella—"

His eyes were kind now, but she knew he wasn't ready to give in, so she pushed harder. "Greg, you spent so much time trying to shield me, more than I will ever know. But I don't want that to be the basis of our relationship. I do not want to be in a relationship where you are constantly defending me while I sit back and do nothing, nor do I want the opposite. I want to walk beside you." She cupped his face with her other hand. "And I think you want that too. I think you want someone who can be your partner and teammate. I want to be that, so let me."

He hung his head, his forehead resting against hers as she wrapped her arms around him. Greg clung to her and his voice quivered as he spoke. "What you're asking from me is impossible. I want you to be my partner, but to know that you might get hurt … I can't."

"But I would rather be injured and heal tomorrow than lose you today. You need to learn to trust me."

Greg's hands slid up her back. "I do trust you. It's never been a case of me not trusting you. It's been a case of wanting more for you, of caring for you, and worrying about you. That is my love for you." He pulled her closer. "But I do trust you, I've always trusted you."

"Then if you trust me, let me be with you, please. We will be better together than apart. You need to realize I can take care of myself. You need to have faith in me, just like I have faith in you to help me if I need it. Letting me stand beside you doesn't mean that you can't still protect me. It means that you believe I will be capable enough to tell you when I need help, and when I can defend myself and stand on my own. I also have to believe the same thing with you. You may be immortal, but I know that doesn't mean you're invincible." She ran her fingers over his nape. "I will not lose you Greg, I refuse to." Her voice wavered. "Please don't make me rely on someone else to take me there because you cannot believe in me."

His eyes hardened. "You would go that far?"

"To bring you back home to me, yes. I can deal with your anger. I can deal with hurting you, or even betraying you, but I cannot deal with losing you."

He balled his hands behind her back and spoke under his breath. "If only tying you up would work."

"It wouldn't be any fun if you weren't here to enjoy it with me." Daniella smirked. Her hands traced the strong muscles of his back as the smile died from her lips. "Please. *Please.*"

Greg cupped her cheek as he leaned forward, placing a soft kiss on her forehead, then the side of her face. He breathed in her scent. "It seems I don't really have much of a choice."

"You do." Daniella traced the waistband of his pants, drawing a small gasp from him. "It would mean the world to me to have your blessing."

"Vixen," he grumbled as he nibbled on her neck.

Daniella sighed and surrendered herself to him. She made quick work of his pants and boxers, pushing and kicking them off. Greg ripped her towel away and they fell into one another.

She moaned in their kiss as he spread her thighs, fitting himself between them. He sucked her nipple and she arched her back. Her hands were full of his body, scratching his back as she tried to pull him closer. Daniella rolled her hips forward, but he stopped her.

"Please," she said, needing both his answer and his body.

He took her lips again and she wrapped her legs around his waist as he carried her into the shower. Greg turned on the water and pinned her against the wall. His fingers found their way to her slick core and he grunted at her wetness.

Daniella moaned, tearing her mouth from his to smother kisses over his skin. "Please," she begged again. When he said nothing, she bit his neck.

Her only warning was a growled moan before he shoved himself into her with such force she lost her breath. Her eyes rolled back. He snarled and rammed inside her over and over. She clung to him as he filled her so completely. He was ruthless with her, and she loved it. She wanted this, him, forever, always. Greg gripped her hips hard as he drove deeper, and she chanted, "Please, please, please."

He moaned and kissed her, sliding his tongue into her mouth, flicking, rubbing, wrapping it around hers just as his cock drove her insane. Daniella gripped his back, her nails scratching, biting into the flesh. She needed more. He hissed, squeezed her breasts, rolling and pinching her nipples between his fingers, drawing long cries from her lungs.

"Please! Please," she begged, one last time.

Greg tugged her head back before plunging his teeth into her neck. She held him there, her body writhing, jerking against his, her hips moving and circling uncontrollably as he drove her higher. Then she screamed, clamping down on his cock as her orgasm soared through her. He gripped her ass, angling her hips, pounding faster, *deeper,* and then he threw his head back, shouting as he filled her with his come.

For a long time, neither of them moved. The only sounds were those of their harsh breaths and the steady stream of water. Eventually she rubbed his back, drawing spirals on his skin. He nuzzled the crook of her neck and pulled out of her.

"Greg—"

"I trust you," he said softly, "and I love you." He laced his fingers through hers, holding their hands beside her head. "Do you feel this?"

Something wrapped around their hands, tingling. It was similar to what she felt when he was near her, except stronger, more potent. "Yes."

"Can you connect to it somehow?"

She held onto the way his ability felt, a vibration that was purely Greg. It bonded to something at the very core of her being. Calling on the spirit of darkness for a point of release, she morphed her energy, allowing it to twine around his own.

He gasped, staring at their clasped hands in wonder. "Amazing."

"What does it feel like?"

"It's odd. It feels like mist, but energized, like it's wrapped in an electric pulse." His eyes focused on her now. "This"—he squeezed her hand—"this is ours. If you need me, you call me this way."

"But, if you're in the middle of a fight—"

"You call," he said sternly, his fingers tracing her cheek. "And if I need you, I will reach out to you. Okay?"

"Thank you." Daniella pulled his head to hers and kissed him.

He sighed when they broke apart. "Have you come up with some sort of plan of how to use your abilities?"

She nodded.

Dropping a kiss on her palm, he turned toward the soap. "Good, we can go over it together, after this."

Greg poured the soap into his hands and ran them over her body, working it into a lather. She melted into his hands. His touch wasn't sexual, but it was intimate and warm. When he finished and she had rinsed, she washed him, bringing a serene smile to his lips.

Greg rested his forehead against hers and closed his eyes. Daniella wrapped her arms around his neck. "I don't know what's going on in your mind right now, but remember that I love you and I'm happy here with you."

"I know," he said. His muscular arms enveloped her and she sighed in his embrace. "When this is all over, I want to take you somewhere, just you and I." He rubbed his nose against hers. "We have a lot to figure out together."

She grinned. "I'd say we've made a bit of headway with that though, haven't we?"

"Fucking finally," he breathed, a moment before his lips met hers in a sweet kiss.

19

The house filled with boisterous energy as Greg's battle officers arrived. They shouted over one another, clapped their hands while they laughed, and teased each other endlessly. Under different circumstances, Daniella would have been overjoyed. But for now, the most she could muster was a small smile. Perhaps when she had lived a hundred years and fought countless wars beside these people, she too would value comradery over impending chaos.

The room quieted to a few murmurs and the soft buzz of a speaker as she and Greg entered. Sixteen people sat in attendance, many of whom Daniella had never met. But it was clear they respected Greg as their leader by how they straightened and gave him their full attention. It was also clear in how their eyes wandered over her skeptically.

That reaction pleased her. Greg had found an excellent group of people, and their love and loyalty filled her heart with a sense of pride for her mate. She didn't want them to welcome her because Greg commanded them to, or out of respect for him. She wanted to earn it.

"Everyone." Greg paused and kissed her hand. "I'd like to introduce you to Daniella, my mate." The smile on his face was just for her, tender and kind. It spread through her body, leaving warmth in its wake.

Greg took a seat at the head of the table while she took her place beside him on the arm of the chair. His hand came to rest on her lower back and he caressed her spine, sending small tingles of energy through her system.

"She's human," one of Greg's warriors challenged, his near black eyes unforgiving.

Daniella read the message loud and clear. *You don't belong here. You'll break far too easily.*

Her eyes narrowed as she answered. "Yes, I am human, but that will not stop me from joining tonight's battle."

The man gave her a cruel, twisted smile that made Daniella straighten in the chair.

Greg's fingers paused on her back as he tensed. "Darius—"

Daniella squeezed his thigh under the table. *Let me,* she projected to him as their eyes met, and then she turned back to his people. "It's clear to me you all share a close bond. You work as a team, a family, and I recognize it may be strange for me to be here, as many of you do not know me. So let me take this opportunity to make myself and my presence here very clear."

Her gaze flickered to Greg's and she couldn't stop the smile that spread over her lips. "I love Greg, and while I am new to the way your world works, I am not ignorant of its dangers. I do not expect any of you to respect me, or treat me the way you treat Greg, as a proxy. However, I expect you to work with me because I am here for the same reasons you are. Now, are there any more questions of my loyalty or assumed fragility, or can we focus on why we're all here today?"

Darius held up his hands in a small retreat, and Luke and Mya gave her cheeky smiles of approval.

Greg's voice was thick behind her, filled with pride. He gave Daniella's hip a soft squeeze. "Mya, if you'd please," he said, not wanting to dwell.

Mya pulled open the map on the projection screen. "The coordinates lead here." She tapped on an area full of foliage. "There's one road in and out. The location is only accessible on foot, so we'll have to leave our vehicles behind. This"—she traced a path on the map—"is the route we'll take. It leads to an unmarked cavern where Zachariah will be waiting for us."

"I believe their plan is to force us into the cavern and overwhelm us from there. Because we're unsure of the structure or size, your teams will stay behind. If we have too many people, we'll risk losing someone during the fight," Greg said in a measured tone, but

Daniella could feel the vibration that hummed through his body. She laced her fingers with his, lending him her strength as he continued.

"Daniella will be our first line of defense." The temperature of the room dropped a few degrees, but Greg pushed on. "Her abilities will help weaken the vampires if she doesn't outright kill them. After that, you all can have your fun."

"What do we do if Zachariah runs? Will you hunt him down like usual?" someone asked.

"No," Greg answered, making everyone's head swivel in shock, including Daniella's. "While I would like to rip his arms from their sockets and use them to bash his head in, this isn't about me. What's important here is to make sure he doesn't make it out alive. However that happens, and by whoever's hand, doesn't matter to me."

He directed his attention to the speaker system. "Michael, Cara, and Isaac, have you positioned your teams at the victims' addresses?"

"Yes," they answered, one after another.

"Good, there's one last thing I need to address," Greg said. "We have reason to believe that Zachariah has the power to copy another's ability if he drinks their blood."

A wave of shock and fury flew through the room. Several of the warriors' eyes widened, and some gasped and cursed, while others sat silent, their lips drawn in a tight line.

"We also have reason to believe that there will be several traps waiting for us which we are not used to. I have two priorities: the safety of all of my people, and ending this war. I leave the decision of adding someone to the circle to each of you." Greg indicated his team with a wave of his hand. "If you believe we can convert a vampire from Zachariah's way to ours, bring them with you and we will discuss after this is over. But if you do not, kill them."

The command hung in the air, making it heavy as each officer shouldered its weight.

Merida spoke, breaking through the silence. "When do we leave?"

"Forty-five minutes and in groups of three. Provide area reports in fifteen-minute increments," Greg said. "Merida, Mya, and Dom, you go first. Scout and radio back if you see anything."

Once the meeting ended, the team shifted and broke into smaller groups. They wandered the house, visited Greg's armory—which Daniella had yet to see herself—or congregated in the kitchen to feast on the refreshments.

Greg brought her around to meet each member of his team. They were pleasant and most were happy for the two of them. Some even shared stories of how Greg had saved their lives, making him blush. He tried to drag her away, but she'd dug in her heels until he squirmed from the praise. It was nice. Familial.

Luke's arm wrapped around her shoulder and Daniella laughed, giving him a hug. "Hey you!"

"Hey." He smiled. "I still can't believe you're coming with us tonight."

She wagged a finger at him. "Before you start with your big brother protective crap, I have a reason to."

He raised his hands in surrender. "You'll hear none of that from me."

"You're not going to argue?" Daniella raised an eyebrow.

Luke cocked his head to the side. "No?"

"What is wrong with you?"

Luke laughed, but the sound seemed forced to her. "I'm just happy for the two of you, Dani. If Greg says it's okay and you can help him somehow, I'm all for it."

"Luke what's going—"

"Hey," Mya interrupted, "we're about to head out, but I left a bag on the bed for you in that room." She pointed to the left. "Go through it before you meet up with us, okay?"

Daniella nodded and the two shared a hug. "Stay safe, please," she whispered to her friend.

Mya laughed. "Don't worry, I'll be just fine."

When Daniella turned back to address Luke, he was gone. She searched the first floor for him but couldn't find him anywhere. What was going on with him, and why was he hiding it from her?

With a sigh, she gave up and went to investigate Mya's gift. Searching through the bag, she pulled out a small note with jagged, curved writing.

"Thank you for listening and still deciding to come. Wear these. They'll help you stay as fluid as possible. -Mya."

The bag contained a black tank top, leather jacket, pants, and combat boots. She chuckled and changed into the apparel. Flipping her hair from under the top, Daniella stared at herself in the floor-length mirror. She looked strong, dangerous. *Fierce.*

A tingle rippled over her body and in the mirror she saw Greg, his gaze dark and wicked. "Don't," she whispered.

He chuckled. "As if that was ever a possibility." With each step towards her, he rolled his hips. A memory of just how skillful those hips were flashed through her mind and she moaned.

Greg's nostrils flared as he breathed her in and then his hands were everywhere, sliding up her shirt, under her bra to squeeze her breast while his fingers came to cup her through the leather pants.

"Greg, please," she panted as he undid the button and lowered the zipper. "Do you know how hard it was to get these on?"

"I'll help you after," he huffed in her ear, "but I need you, *now*."

Her head lolled back as he rubbed her nipple. She pushed her hips against his when Greg slipped his fingers under her thong and over her labia, teasing her lips. Then he rubbed her clit and his fingers slipped down, spreading her lips. He moaned. "Fuck, you're so wet, Ella."

She ground against him, trapped between his heady strokes and hard cock. He moaned and glided his fingers inside her. She twisted, and Greg took her lips in a passionate kiss. He swallowed her fervent moans, his tongue tangling with hers.

Daniella shoved her pants down, widening her legs to give him more access. He rewarded her by sliding his fingers deeper while he fucked her mouth, sending another pool of wetness to her core.

She gripped his hair with one hand while she fought to unbutton his pants.

Greg lifted his mouth from hers and smacked her ass hard, making her whimper and moan. "Stay quiet for me," he commanded, and then he dropped to his knees, replacing his fingers with his mouth. He sucked her pussy, then licked between her lips before delving into her core.

Daniella covered her mouth, resting her forehead against the mirror to quiet her moans while he ravaged her. Greg ate her like a starving man, and when he stood, she was barely holding herself together. She turned her head in time to see his cock spring free before he filled her with one solid thrust.

He clamped his hand over her mouth as she cried. Squeezing her hips, Greg pulled her back against him with each thrust. Daniella grabbed a hold of his nape, her nails scratching his skin as he pounded harder inside her.

Greg traced her ear with his tongue. "Look at us in the mirror," he moaned. "Watch me as I fuck you."

She watched his cock glide in and out of her, watched as her pussy swallowed every inch of him. He guided her hand down to where they were joined and pulled out of her until only the tip of his shaft was left inside. Wrapping their hands around his cock, he gasped in her ear.

"Do you feel how drenched I am? That's all you, baby, all you," he growled as he slid into her again, inch by glorious inch. "That's it, take it. Take all of me."

And she did. Fuck, she did. Daniella wanted to swallow him whole.

He ruined her against that mirror. Greg squeezed her breasts while his lips latched on to hers to drink every cry he tore from her. When he lifted his head from hers again, he moved to her neck and bit her. She closed her eyes, pressing her hand against her mouth as she tried to smother her scream. Still he moved, and still she took him.

She grabbed hold of him anywhere, everywhere, holding on for dear life as he fucked her, *possessed* her. He forced her hand to the edge of the mirror, holding it in his own, adding the sound of the mirror rocking against the wall to the passionate slap of his hips against her ass. Daniella came so hard that she saw stars, and with one last maddening thrust, Greg followed her into the abyss.

When she exited the bathroom, Greg was sitting on the bed with a dagger on each side of him.

"What's this?" she asked.

"They're for you. We're too fast for guns or most modern weapons." He shuddered as he breathed. "I thought these would work well for you."

Standing in front of him, she rested her hands on his shoulders while he wrapped his arms around her. "Thank you."

Greg nuzzled her stomach as she ran her fingers through his hair.

"Are you scared?" she whispered.

He nodded against her stomach and then met her eyes. "I trust you and I believe in you. But yes, I'm still scared. It's something I'll need to work on."

Daniella rubbed his cheek. "Will you let me help you?"

"You already are," he replied, bringing her hand to his lips for a gentle kiss.

The soft beep of an alarm started from his watch, and with a sigh he turned it off and stood. "It's time. Daniella," he began, saying her name as if he savored it, cherished it, "I love you so much. Be safe for me, please."

"I will." She grabbed onto his shirt as he bent to kiss her. "Promise me you will be too."

"I promise."

20

The forest felt like death. Whatever animals had come to this place had died brutally and left a stain on the land. The dirt was tainted with it, and something told Daniella it was not only animals who had lost their lives here. Regardless, the smart creatures knew not to come back, leaving the forest silent. A part of her wanted to reach out, to heal the land and bring it back to its previous glory, but now wasn't the time.

"Are you all right?" Greg asked.

Daniella shuddered but nodded. "They're here and they have been for a very long time."

He squeezed her hand, and for just a moment she leaned into his strength. Then they joined the group and entered the dark cavern.

As they ventured deeper, Daniella called upon the spirit of light to allow her to see, setting her eyes aglow. She didn't feel the spirit of darkness or any warning cultivate within her body. Perhaps it was a sign that the outcome of this battle would be in their favor.

Daniella paused at the entrance of another passageway and used her connection with the spirits to sense. She felt nothing. Merida stood beside her, using her ability to look through items, and also confirmed there to be no threats in the passageway. The group advanced forward, pausing and searching each junction they found this way, only to come up empty. But then they came upon a large opening, and when they exited, they were greeted by Zachariah and his vast army.

"Well, if this isn't a surprise!" Zachariah clapped, Johanna at his side. "I was expecting you, Greg, but bringing Daniella? What an interesting turn of events! I take it you got my message." Zachariah fixed his gaze on Daniella. "Thank you for that friend of yours. Stacy, was it? She was absolutely delicious. I enjoyed her, really, although you were a much better play toy." His smirk deepened. "You didn't scream as much."

Energy flew out from Daniella, so strong it shook the cavern walls, rippling through the space, creating fissures in the ground. She let the full force of the water spirit take her over, a beautiful wave of destruction winding through her body, infusing her with strength and blending with her desire to kill.

Daniella pushed out that intent to every vampire that stood between her and her enemy. They groaned and staggered, but they weren't who she wanted. No, she wanted Zachariah. She wanted to feel his blood boil, for him to become so delirious he couldn't move, couldn't speak, couldn't even scream. She wanted him to know what death felt like, and she wanted it to be at her hand.

In an instant, their group moved as one. Greg launched forward, the others coming in waves as they worked to slay their adversaries.

Zachariah's eyes widened at Daniella's attack. He staggered, but his enhanced strength fought her. She pushed harder, satisfied when he fell back against the wall. But then he grabbed Johanna's wrist and fled down another passageway.

Daniella dashed after him, but the darkness screamed at her. She spun away just in time to avoid a vampire launching himself from the ceiling. With a crazed stare, he ran his tongue over teeth that were much too large for his mouth, like he could *taste* her.

In your dreams.

He swung at her. Daniella dodged his attack, and his next two. His size was a weakness she exploited. When he tried to hit her again, she spun, infusing her kick with a force of air as it hit his gut. He doubled over. Knowing he'd recover quickly, she called on the earth to create vines to tie around his throat. He struggled and ripped them off, but not before she plunged her dagger deep into his skull.

Instinctively, Daniella pulled it out and his lifeless body dropped to the floor in a pool of blood. Her hand shook when the realization hit her. She'd *killed* someone. It was different when she used her abilities.

They could consume her, block out what she'd done in the heat of the moment so her emotions weren't involved. But this? No, this had been done by her hand. But that was what she'd agreed to, wasn't it?

He can't hurt anyone else. None of the people lying here can, and that's what's important. That's why you came here today.

Daniella gripped her dagger tighter and turned away. A blur caught her eye as another vampire sped toward her. She focused on him, tracking his movements. He reached for her. She grabbed his arm, ducked, and flipped him onto his back. Her dagger was in his head the moment he hit the ground. Taking his life hurt her, but she reminded herself why she was there and moved forward with her mission.

Daniella stepped over his body and sprinted to catch up with her team. She froze in front of the field of dead vampires, ones that she helped kill with her abilities, and shuddered.

That pause became her downfall as four vampires surrounded her. Her adrenaline spiked as fear coated her skin, but she shook it off.

Stay calm. Think.

One vampire lurched toward her. Daniella called on her connection with light, blinding the group. She impaled the nearest vampire with her dagger. His body dropped and she used the new path to escape. Daniella jumped over him, but another vampire yanked her back by her hair. Flipping her other dagger, she stabbed him in the gut and twisted. He howled, throwing her to the ground. She scrambled to get up, but wasn't fast enough.

The third vampire pounced on her, his hands around her throat. She squirmed, tried to kick him off, but he was too strong. Daniella released a surge of electricity, sending it through his body. He screamed as she crawled out from underneath him, but then the fourth grabbed her from behind. She tried to electrocute him as well, but he slammed her head into the cavern wall. Pain erupted behind her eyes.

No!

She called upon fire, sending flames to burn his skin, but he hit her again. Her vision clouded as his hot breath huffed against her face.

He's going to bite me. No...

Using her darkness, she called for Greg, begging the connection to reach him. The vampire snarled, but the bite never came. Suddenly, she was free. She turned in time to see Greg rip the man's throat apart. He broke the neck of the gutted vampire before using his sword to behead the one she'd electrocuted.

His red eyes met hers as he stalked toward her.

"Greg—"

He pulled her into his arms, burying his head in her neck.

She clung to him, and after a few deep breaths she whispered, "I'm okay."

His shirt was covered in something sticky, and when she finally lifted her head, Daniella realized it was blood. “Greg!” She pushed at his chest, running her hands over his shirt. “Where are you hurt?”

“It’s not my blood,” he bit out. Greg swiped at her temple, a look of pure rage coming over him. He growled.

She gasped as she realized he wasn’t the only one covered in blood. Her hands, arms, even her chest were coated in the horrible red spray, and now she was bleeding from her forehead.

He pressed a gentle kiss to the gash and then traced it with his tongue. She sighed at his touch. The heaviness in her head cleared as he healed her, bringing her back to the present. Daniella moved to pull away from him, but he held her still.

“We don’t have time—” she began.

“We do. They’re all dead or will be soon.” Greg ran his fingers through her hair. “We’d cleared this area of vampires. The ones that attacked you came from outside. Marcus and Antoine are making sure that area is clear as well.”

“And Zachariah? Did you kill him?”

He shook his head. “I came for you first.”

“Then let’s go.” She took his hand, but he pulled her back.

“Ella—”

“I’m okay, I promise. We have to kill him. Let’s go.”

Marcus and Antoine appeared beside them.

“We’ve dispatched the vampires outside,” Marcus said.

"Good. Guard the entrance. The team will explore any channels they find for five minutes and then work their way back to you."

While the others paired off to carry out Greg's orders, Mya, Luke, Merida, Dominick, Darius, Jason, and Anna stayed with them. Their group set off to find Zachariah and Johanna and put an end to this war.

They made it to an opening with two different passageways. Before they could take another step forward, Luke took off, taking the passage to the right.

"Luke!" they yelled out in unison, but he was already gone.

"What the fuck is his problem?" Mya hissed.

"I don't know," Greg growled in reply. "Mya, go get him. Dom, Merida, and Anna go with her. Drag his ass back to the entrance if you have to."

They nodded and took off behind him. Daniella stared after them, trying to make sense of Luke's actions. While nothing had warned her of that path, the sudden separation filled her with unease.

Greg squeezed her hand. "They'll be fine, I promise."

She met his gaze and allowed his words to reassure her. Then together, they took the path to the left.

"There's something down here," Jason said as he moved to take the lead.

Daniella and Greg followed behind him, with Darius at the end.

"Jay, we have two minutes before we have to reconnect with the team," Greg said.

Jason nodded.

They continued walking and then reached another passageway with a single beam of light at the end. Jason took a step forward and Daniella's eyes widened as dread filled her entire body. Warning bells howled in her mind and she flew forward.

"Wait!" she called out. She pulled Jason back just as a metal click reverberated in the chamber.

"Daniella!" Greg reached for her, but it was too late.

Time slowed as she called on her connection to air. Daniella spread her arms wide, sending a large gust out and around her body a second before the wall exploded and everything went black.

Daniella's cheek was wet. Someone was screaming and shaking her violently. Each jostle made the sharp pain in her head worse and she groaned. The shaking stopped as strong arms wrapped around her. Daniella soaked in the warmth, and when she breathed in his smell, she smiled.

"Greg?" She opened her eyes and his hold tightened. Daniella wrapped her arms around him and stroked his back. "What's wrong?"

"What's wrong?" he shouted. He shook her hard, making her groan again. At the noise, Greg pulled her head to his shoulder as tears rolled down his face. "You ran into a fucking explosion, Daniella! Why would you ever, ever—"

Dazed, she blinked once, twice. Realizing they were outside, she forced herself to remember what happened. With wide eyes, she tried to pull herself back and check him for injuries, but he refused to let her go. "Are you okay?"

"What? Yes, but—"

"Good." She relaxed in his embrace and smiled. "Then it was worth it."

"Worth it? I swear to the gods—"

"If I may," Jason interrupted, "she saved all of us. Thank you, Daniella."

"You did good," Darius said, his expression tight.

Greg growled, giving the man a death glare. He was shaking, Daniella realized. She squeezed his back and nuzzled the crook of his neck.

"You scared the hell out of me," Greg bit out, even as his hands smoothed down her spine carefully.

"I'm sorry, but I just … I knew that was it, what the spirits warned me about and I—"

His eyes glowed red. "That doesn't mean you should run in and sacrifice yourself!"

"I know, but I knew I would be okay. And I am okay. Counteracting the blast just took a lot out of me. But if you're safe, that's all that matters."

He hugged her tighter, but then his head snapped up. A moment later someone yelled as they ran through the trees toward them. "We found them!"

"What?" Daniella cocked her head to the side. "Found who? Greg, what's going on?"

"That wasn't the only explosion," Greg said, his eyes fixed on the trees.

"What?" she gasped.

Greg lifted her in his arms, carrying her as he followed down the path. "The entire cave system collapsed. Everyone returned to the main entrance except for Mya, Merida, Dom, and Luke. But if they found them, that means they're okay—"

He stopped dead in his tracks and Daniella gaped at the sight. They were there, standing, moving about just fine, but the surprise was the multiple groups of women in various states of undress who sat around them. Their skin was covered in blood, dirt, and filth. Countless wounds marred their flesh, alongside bruises from what looked like weeks of attacks.

"Put me down," Daniella ordered. When Greg didn't move immediately, she smacked his arm to get his attention. "Put me down!"

He did, and then he helped her toward the women.

She took off her jacket, wrapping it around the nearest woman as Merida approached. "What can we do?" Daniella asked.

"They need food, water." Merida shook her head, her expression strained as she fought to keep herself from losing control. "I don't even think half of them realize they're alive."

"Okay." Daniella opened her heart to the spirits. She asked for rain, and it came as a gentle sprinkle over the area. She wanted to do more, to ask the earth to bring them food, but she couldn't. This act alone took everything she had.

Many of the women didn't move at first, didn't even seem to register they were outside. But slowly, one shifted, then another. Tears fell down their faces, mixing in with the rainwater as they tilted their heads back. Finally, they drank deep gulps. Some were so thirsty that they choked on the liquid, but even then they tried to swallow more, as if they hadn't drunk for days.

It broke her heart.

"What happened? Where did you find them?" Greg asked, his voice thick.

"When we ran after Luke, I saw another chamber inside," Merida said. "At first I thought it was a group of vampires that were planning to ambush us, but then we found them." Her gaze flickered to the women and she spoke in a hushed tone. "They were used for blood and anything else he wanted. Some of them aren't even human, Greg, and judging by their conditions, they've been down there for a long time."

"How did you get out?" Daniella asked.

"Luke. I'm not sure how, but he led us out. Greg, something happened to him in that cave. I've never seen him like this. We can take care of the girls, but please, go help him. He's over there." Merida tilted her head to the left.

When Daniella and Greg approached Luke, he was looking over the women but his eyes were glazed, unfocused, like he didn't really see them. He seemed to be searching for something, or someone.

"Luke?" Greg called to him, getting his attention.

"Johanna. Have you seen Johanna?" Luke's eyes were red, wild. He looked over another woman before shaking his head and moving to the next. "I have to find her."

"Luke," Greg said carefully, "the last time we saw her, she was with Zachariah."

"I know!" he shouted, but then his voice dropped to a whisper. "But she could be here. She could be here. I have to find her."

"Luke," Daniella tried, "I don't think she's here."

"Then where is she?" Luke's voice boomed, making the women around them jump. He ran up to Greg and clutched his shirt. "Tell me we killed him. Tell me he's dead, at least. Please!"

Greg shook his head.

"Someone has to have seen something! What direction did they go off to? Where are they, Greg?" His voice wavered as he choked back tears.

Greg squeezed his wrists. "Luke, they escaped in the explosions. We don't know where they've gone. We're looking, but we have to take care of the people here first," he explained gently, like a parent speaking to a child.

Luke hung his head. "No!" he screamed, falling to his knees. "No, no, no."

Daniella wrapped her arms around Luke's shaking and sobbing form, as did Greg.

"Luke," she tried again. He lifted his head to her voice, but instead of her best friend, she saw a broken shell of a man. "Can you tell us why you're looking for Johanna?"

Luke's eyes were drowning in despair as he met her own. "She's my mate, Dani."

At his words, Daniella and Greg drew back. Her eyes widened and she gasped. She turned to Greg to see a mixture of fury, regret, and horror blanket his face.

Luke wept and wailed, his anguish seeping into her soul as he splintered and fell apart. "She's my mate, and he took her."

The End

Acknowledgements

To Emily, thank you for all of your feedback and suggestions. You really made my book shine!

To my editor, Ellen, thank you so much for all you've done. You helped me keep my voice, and really brought it back in the places where my edits went a little overboard. You also made this easy for me, and your support, guidance, and assistance made me feel like I had someone in my corner.

To my cover designer, LJ, I don't know what magic you have over there but thank you for sprinkling it on my cover. It's gorgeous!

To you. Yes! You! Thank you so much for reading my novel. Knowing that you took the the time to read it is beyond amazing to me. You help every author to move forward, to write their next book, to publish, to celebrate. That's all you. So thank you again, take care, and I hope to see you on my next book!

Author's Bio

Melissa Cummins has been writing for as long as she can remember, first poetry, then music, and now novels. Her work has always focused on the heart, creating deep emotion and loving bonds. But perhaps the Florida heat is to blame for her love of steamy paranormal romance.

When Melissa isn't writing or dreaming up her next scene, she's fiddling around with magic. Melissa is a huge mythology buff, with a love of all things supernatural, paranormal, and steeped in lore and fantasy. She can also be found gardening, singing, dancing, or on the rare chance, up late at night contemplating space and the universe with a large cup of tea.

Want to keep up with Melissa? Follow her here:

Or visit her website: https://melissacummins.com

Made in the USA
Columbia, SC
30 September 2021